"The Book you are about to read will cause you to expand your own imagination regarding biblical characters, as well as appreciate their biblical roles. In writing biblical historical fiction, the greatest danger is to insert that which would be contrary to Bible truth. The writer has effectively caught the interest of the reader through the storyline while avoiding the above mentioned error. Also, he has introduced us to middle eastern culture that is often overlooked by western eyes and minds. He has introduced typical human conflicts, painful pregnancy and childbirth experiences as well as common everyday personal challenges. I am a wide reader of biblical and non-biblical fiction but I do not recall ever reading a story line with Joseph of Nazareth as the main character.

"I trust you will enjoy your reading and when you do, remember, I told you this would happen."

Jim Alley, 54 years Pastor and Global Mission Worker

"I really enjoyed reading Joseph of Nazareth. It is nice for the time when I am preparing for bed -- to focus on Jesus. I often contemplate the days of Jesus times, local culture, school system, families and what they (Joseph and Mary) were doing between Jesus's birth and year 12 and, then, later when Jesus began his earthly ministry. What did it mean to be a carpenter in the first century Palestine? What happened to the gifts the family received from the Maggi from the East? What else happened that is not portrayed in the Gospels? How was life for a relatively large family in those days? It may well be that it looked the way the author is portraying – uncommon love, faith, friendships, accusations, difficult wider family relations, and forgiveness above all. And especially, what happened to other people in the Gospel story. That is the beauty of this book."

Branko Bjelajac, MDiv, ThM, MA, MSc, Dr.Sc. (PhD). Author of **The Bible among the Serbs** (Serbian), **Protestantism in Serbia** (Serbian), **The Believers in Christ** (English) and **Who are Evangelical Christians** (Serbian).

Joseph of Nazareth

Joseph of Nazareth

A Story of Uncommon Love and Faith

by

George D. Cooper

Scripture quotations are taken from the *Holy Bible* New Living Translation, Second Edition (NLT2) copyright ©1996, 2004. Used by permission of Tyndale Charitable Trust

Cover design by J. R. Cooper

Published by WordCooper8

Printed by DiggyPOD, Inc., in the United States of America.

First printing, 2021.

 george.cooper.75054/

or write to me at WordCooper8@gmail.com

Dedication

To Joann,

Wife

Mother of three

Grandmother of 16

Encourager

Singer

Teacher

Editor

Writer

Graphic Artist

Most of all,

Best Friend.

Contents

x

Forward

Please be aware that "Joseph of Nazareth" is mostly fictional. Scripture says very little about the man who was the earthly father of Jesus. All we have is a genealogy, a few proclamations from an angel, and a few scenes where he is involved. There are no words of his recorded. There are, however, several strong qualities we can attribute to him, some from what is said about him and some from what is not said.

The only description of Joseph is Matthew 1:19 where he is described as 'righteous' or 'just' or 'upright' or 'good' depending on the translation.

This book began one Christmas when I heard a teenage girl comment, "Joseph was a wimp." Not responding outwardly, I felt strong disagreement. Thus, began a study of Joseph to disprove her perception. From this came the idea of a short story on his life.

The planned short story would not stay short, however, as new ideas and pictures of his life came to mind. It is simply my view of how Joseph's life might have transpired.

As you read, I trust you will gain a new appreciation of what Joseph and Mary must have faced in the rearing of their son, Jesus. And, more important, learn how they responded to the challenges they faced.

There are many assumptions made in the Christmas story about Joseph and Mary that are contradicted here. The changes made to the traditional story are made with biblical support. On the other hand, some new assumptions are made that cannot be supported by scripture, but are not contradicted as nothing is revealed about them in scripture.

The purpose of this book is to make Joseph a real living person by telling his story in his own words. It is not strictly a representation of the way people lived in those days. Therefore, much about dress, customs and other cultural issues are left out. Joseph is telling his own story and like us, his culture was so much a part of him that he would not normally speak about it. As someone said about culture, "The last thing a fish will ever know, is that it lives in water."

George Cooper

1

The Cradle

"Oh, Joseph, it's beautiful! I've never seen anything so lovely. When did you do this? How did you..."

Mary's response overwhelmed me. Finally, I sputtered, "Well, it did take me a year...in my spare time...I wanted it to be something very special."

Even if it wasn't special to others, I considered it a work of art—all wood, carefully fitted joints, no glue, no nails. Finished with natural oils, and hand rubbed. It almost glowed. I had loved it to perfection.

Earlier that day, after quitting my carpentry work for the day, I cleaned up and dressed in my best tunic and a robe. Covering the handmade cradle with a clean, white tunic, I left for Mary's house. Her parents had invited me for supper to celebrate our betrothal and possibly begin making wedding plans.

Almost everyone in Mary's family showed up for the occasion! Perhaps I shouldn't have been surprised, but then I didn't know what to expect. I assumed it would be just her parents and Mary and me. Nervously, I greeted everyone awkwardly clutching the cradle under my arm. The giggling and whispering I heard seemed to center on, "What did Joseph make this time?" You see bringing gifts wasn't unusual for me. But this gift was much larger than normal.

When the greetings and blur of new faces were finally over, I handed the gift to Mary. The puzzled look in her eyes said, *What's this?*

"Look and see!" I croaked.

As she took the gift, I glanced around at the family members I had just met. All eyes were on Mary and me. Their whispering grew louder and I panicked! *Why did she have to have such a big family?* Suddenly I was overcome with self-consciousness. My knees began to knock and my hands started sweating. Thankfully my long tunic covered my jitters and gave me a place to wipe my hands! *What's wrong with me?* Normally calm and unexcitable, I suddenly realized the reason for my panic. Perhaps this wasn't a proper gift for a bride-to-be. *Is it too bold? Too suggestive?* I hadn't talked to anyone about the cradle for fear that Mary would find out. *What if she is embarrassed?*

As Mary carefully unwrapped the gift, these thoughts raced through my mind. For months I had dreamed about the joy, the ecstasy of this occasion. Never once had I thought it might be considered improper. But now...

The time it took Mary to uncover the cradle seemed an eternity. It was so long ago now I can't remember everything that was said, but I'll never forget the emotion. Mary looked at the cradle glowing in her hands, her eyes wide in astonishment. She looked at me, then back at the cradle. She started to say something then stopped and looked at her parents; then her eyes went back to the cradle. Finally, her mother broke the silence. "Mary, perhaps you should thank Joseph," she prompted.

At last, Mary looked fully at me. She blushed, but her eyes were bright. Suddenly, her face lit up with the beautiful smile I loved so much. Her face glowed! It was easy to see she loved the cradle. Only then did I take my eyes off Mary and glance at her parents. Relief washed over me when they nodded with approval. I looked back at Mary. She really didn't need to say anything, but once she started, the words tumbled out. After telling me how much she loved the cradle and how beautiful it was she added, "You make such sacrifices for me, Joseph. I don't deserve them. This is the loveliest cradle I've ever seen. But...for me? You could sell it and get a fortune!"

I rarely think of the right words in the heat of the moment, but this time, somehow, they came. "Dear Mary," I said quietly, "if selling that piece of wood could make me as rich as a king, it wouldn't give me as much pleasure as seeing the look on your face at this moment. You're my queen! You make me a king by accepting me and the small gifts I make for you." I heard a few snickers from her nephew and brother-in-law, followed by a sound like somebody got poked in the ribs, but it didn't matter anymore.

———————

It all began when Mary and I were pledged to be married. Even before the pledging, I thought Mary was special. She was sincere and mature for her age—a thoughtful person—yet at the same time...happy. When I saw her at the community well drawing water, she reminded me of the story of Rebecca drawing water for Isaac's servant and animals. Mary would help anyone, graciously and with love. When I thought about it, I couldn't understand why her parents chose me to be her husband. Mary, of course, had little to say in the matter. But despite the differences in our ages and temperaments, she never talked about wishing it was different—at least that I know of. Anyway, that would have been unnatural for her. Simply put, she was extra special, but just how special I discovered sometime later.

Since Mary was young when we were pledged, we had to wait to be betrothed. That was easy for Mary. It was just a matter of growing up. But for me the time moved very slowly—I wasn't getting any younger! As time passed, I dreamed of the day Mary would become my wife. In spite of my impatience, she was worth the wait. I was the most fortunate man in the world! God had done a wonderful thing for me.

During this waiting period, I learned to love Mary much more than was usual. Normally pledges were made when children were young and, often, the future mates didn't even know about it until they were teenagers. They might even dislike each other! For example, if a young girl found out who she was to marry and went to her mother and asked, "Do I hav'ta marry Joash? He's such a bore!" the standard reply was, "Yes, your father and I chose him a long time ago. He comes from a good family."

Our pledge was different from the start. Since my parents were no longer living, the agreement was made between Mary's parents and me. I was an adult and even had my own business. And Mary was the person I wanted to share my life with. Often during the waiting time I went out of my way to walk by her house, hoping to catch a glimpse of her, to watch her work. When I saw her, my heart would skip a beat. When she smiled shyly at me, it was all I could do to keep from gamboling around like a lamb! Mary was always on my mind. I dreamed about her while doing chores around the little house that would be our home and was also my carpentry shop. I thought about her while working, making work a pleasure. It was during these times of dreaming and thinking that the idea came to me. I would make Mary small gifts in my spare time. Things she could use after we were married. It seemed a good idea except, well, except for time and resources.

Now I was a good carpenter, even if I do say so myself. Perhaps not the best, but good and honest. In spite of this, the rich townspeople always seemed to go to the wealthy carpenters, never realizing that they could get just as good a job from me for a lot less money. I suppose they had to keep up their image. So I stayed poor doing jobs for the common people who mostly paid with a chicken, some produce, or something else useful. The result was that I spent all the daylight hours at work for others. Thus, most of the objects I made for Mary had to be small—things like a spoon from olive wood or little bowls from wood left over from a paying job. However small, these gifts also served as a good excuse to visit her. Of course, visiting Mary and her parents often meant a free meal! And there was an added bonus—my visits and gifts seemed to please her parents.

Every time I gave Mary a gift, I apologized for it being so small—why, I would have given her the moon if I could! But Mary was always gracious. "You are too kind to me. You don't have to give me things to show your love. I see it in everything you do. Joseph, you are so-o-o different from other men." Well, this kind of talk only made me want to do more for her.

Then came the big idea. A cradle! I would make a cradle and surprise her with it on our betrothal day.

Accomplishing this project turned out to be both a joy and a struggle. Our betrothal was almost a year away. That seemed like enough time, but I still had to make a living. So, I worked on the cradle at night by the light of a small bowl of olive oil with a wick.

It took me several weeks to plan the cradle—to think through and draw up a simple, yet elegant design. Each piece of wood had to be carefully chosen, each joint precisely made. Then the hard work began, putting all the pieces together.

As the cradle began to take shape, my excitement grew. During my normal work day, time seemed to drag on and on. But at night, when I could work on the cradle, the hours literally flew. And, as the months passed, I worried and wondered if I would finish it on time.

This cradle would be an expression of my commitment to and love for Mary. I saw it—a symbol of our love—lasting long beyond the births of our children. It would become a treasured possession to be passed down for generations.

Well, as you already know, I did finish the cradle on time and I think Mary loved it more than I did.

2

The Angry Carpenter

I moved to Nazareth as a young man soon after my parents died. Even though the village of Nain had been home for most of my life, I wanted to leave. As the only child, I felt the loss of my parents keenly. Nain held too many memories, too many struggles—I needed a new start. So one day I packed up everything I owned, put it on a small cart and set off to find my fortune. Actually, all I wanted was work.

Dragging the cart behind me, I lamented the past years...born in Bethlehem, son of a poor carpenter who was always looking for work just as I was. Tired, sad and discouraged, I remember lifting my hand toward the heavens and crying, "God, I'm tired...Oh, God, help me! Give me something I can do!" Then with my head down and both hands pulling the cart, I trudged on.

Much later in the day as I was wheeling the cart into Nazareth, I happened upon a donkey drawn cart broken down in the middle of the road. I offered to repair the cart and the owner paid me for my work. *Was this a sign from God?* I wondered. So I asked the cart owner, "Is there any place a poor carpenter could settle in this village?" He looked surprised, but then said, "You can stay in my house." He looked at my small cart, perhaps feeling sorry for me, and added, "For all I care you can have it! I'm leaving this place and hope to never see it again!" He turned abruptly and, with a crack of his whip, started off in a cloud of dust.

"Where...?"

"Next house you come to!" He shouted over his shoulder with a laugh.

That seemed strange until I saw the place, then I laughed. No one in their right mind would have called it a house—it looked like a pile of stones thrown haphazardly together. But it was shelter and I was tired from pulling my cart like a donkey all day. So I stayed, fixed up the shack as best I could and looked for work.

Now, after several years, Nazareth has become home. But when I first arrived, still grieving for my parents, I felt extremely lonely. At first I thought I wouldn't make it. I couldn't shake the loneliness. And, of course, poverty didn't help. It was just proof that I had failed once again—that my decision to move to new surroundings was not the solution to my problems.

On top of that, I blamed God for the Roman occupation of our land. Perhaps it was my animosity that made people avoid me. I don't know. It did seem that people gave me jobs only because they felt sorry for me. That was until James came along and helped me put my life back together.

James was everything I was not. Robust, loud, popular, thin-bearded, broad of body, bright of face. He came to my shop one day shouting, "Hey, Joseph! M'name's James! I hear you need some work!" His rumbling voice startled me—it shook the rafters of my shop! I was surprised, too, by his friendliness. I'd seen him around town. Everyone knew James, he was difficult to miss. But I'd never actually met him.

"I could perhaps take another job." I spoke softly, hesitantly.

"Okay, I tell you what you do. My house—tomorrow a little before sundown. I'll show you what I want. Then you stay and break bread with us."

Astonished at his invitation, I looked up from my work. But before I could say anything else, he boomed, his eyes twinkling, "See you there!" He didn't give me a chance to refuse; he just turned around and walked out. And thus began a special friendship.

Even with James' friendship and help it was still difficult to get enough work to make a decent living. But I made some progress. Little by little I worked on the shack until it actually looked like a house. Modest, but adequate enough to live and work in.

———

I often walked the lanes of Nazareth looking for work. On one such morning I heard a beggar crying out, "Alems! Alems! Alems for ta poor! Alems for ta blind." His voice quivered as he intoned his plea. He was sitting on the ground, legs crossed, eyes closed, his head following the footsteps of the passers-by as if he could see them. I stopped in front of him, pulled out my flat coin purse and dug around trying to find the right coin. At least I hoped that's how it seemed! Finally, I pulled out one small copper coin and put it in the beggar's outstretched hand.

When he felt the coin, he handed it back to me. I was sure he was going to tell me my gift was too small. Instead he said, "Shalom, bro! I can tell you're a good man—yep, God fearin' man, but I shouldn't keep this." His voice had lost some of its quivering.

"What? Why not? You're begging aren't you?"

"Oh, ta be sure, yes, but..." he motioned for me to bend down a little closer, then said softly, "I've got more money in my purse than you do in yours."

Affronted, I countered, "What makes you think that?"

"Well, good sir, I may not be able to see, but I can hear ver' well. I listened careful when you were gettin' your coin out and there was no 'chinkling' of coins. Right?"

"I...I guess that's true," I stammered, "but...hmmm, I'd like to do *something* for you!"

"No one ever does anything for a poor, blind man except give him a coin or two," he mumbled in a quavery voice.

"Well, I'll do something and do it quick, too." I had an idea and rushed off to my shop, anxious to fulfill my vow. Before noon I was back.

"Shalom!"

"Ah, the good man who's poorer than me!"

"Only if you're counting coins," I quipped. "Here's my gift for you, something you can use."

The beggar held out his hand; I put the object in it.

"What is it?"

"See if you can figure it out yourself."

"Well," he said, feeling the wood. "It's a wooden pole, that's clear! Hmm, smooth finish, one end bigger than t'other...a flat piece of wood attached to the smaller end. Hmmm, not as long as a man's leg. Not heavy—seems strong, solid." He paused for a moment. "Well, I suppose I could use it to pull myself up after sittin' here all day. Right?"

"Yes, possibly, but I'm looking at it from a different angle."

"You mean, I have ta stand up?" Reluctantly, he began to pull himself up. As he did, I heard many coins jingling. He groaned suddenly and grabbed his waist as if in pain. I had to grab him to keep him from falling. No wonder he had trouble standing—he'd been in the same position all morning. When he was finally on his feet he said, "Still don't see it."

I laughed. "No, I suppose you wouldn't. It's something to sit on so you won't have to sit on the ground all day."

"Right!" And he promptly sat down on the little one legged stool, accompanied once again by a distinct jingling. Then he turned toward me with a serious look on his face.

"Think people'll still give me money if I'm sittin' on this 'stead of the ground?" he asked. It was funny how his voice quivered only when he talked about begging.

"I don't know, but from the sounds I heard when you were getting up you probably don't really need to beg."

"Shh, not so loud, please!" He looked around to hear if anyone else was nearby. "If I ever hear of someone who needs a carpenter, I'll send 'em to you. What's your name?"

"Joseph."

His countenance fell a little. "Oh, I've heard of you! You're the carpenter who's so angry with the Romans."

This time I looked around to make sure no one had heard *him*. "Not so loud, yourself," I whispered. "Enjoy the seat," I added as I turned to head back home once again.

I heard him say thanks, but my feelings were mixed. I was happy to have helped someone in need, but saddened to learn that I already had a reputation. Perhaps I had been a little too vocal about my dislikes. Unfortunately, I blamed God for my distress. *Why didn't God do something about the Romans? Why did my parents have to die and leave me alone? Why did I have to work so hard and get so little?*

That evening at sundown, feeling unusually down, I walked to James' house. I knew I'd be welcome there...knew I could talk freely there. What a relief it was to have a friend!

3

The Disaster

I was puzzled. After all the excitement of our betrothal day and Mary's joy over my 'work of art,' she left Nazareth. When I asked her mother where she was, I was told Mary had gone to visit her cousin Elizabeth just outside of Jerusalem. *Why had she left so abruptly, so soon after our betrothal? Why didn't she tell me she was leaving?* To stay sane, I tried to convince myself she was so excited about recent events she had rushed to tell her cousin everything that had happened.

It was bad enough that she left so suddenly, but even worse—she stayed with her cousin Elizabeth for three months! Those months seemed like a year and created more doubts in my mind. When she did finally return, I was so happy I could hardly contain my joy. And yet...

I was helping my best friend James put a new roof on his house when Mary arrived. It was late in the day and we were both tired. When James stood up to straighten his back, he noticed a group of travelers coming into town. We both looked for a moment wondering who they might be. I lost interest and went back to work. But James, more curious, continued to watch the group. "Ah ha! Look who I see!" he said suddenly in a teasing voice.

"Who?" I asked, still working.

"Someone you've been pining for."

"Come on, James, let's get this job finished before dark," I muttered with exasperation. This wasn't the first time he'd said he saw Mary. He was a great tease and seemed to take pleasure in seeing the pain on my face when I saw she wasn't there. I figured he was just having fun with me again. Usually I didn't mind, but I was already troubled. His teasing didn't help my doubts.

"I mean it!" He called out, "Hey, Mary, look who's up here!" At that I looked up, too. And there she was! Dusty and beautiful! I was so overcome with joy I couldn't speak.

Mary must have been deep in thought. When she looked up and saw James, she smiled broadly...then she saw me. Her smile faded as I greeted her. "Welcome back!" was all I managed to squeak out. "See you later?" I added, hesitantly. She just nodded. For a moment she looked like she'd been caught stealing ripe dates from a neighbor's tree. James joked, "Joseph! Seeing you must have put impure thoughts into her head." He laughed. "Ah, she'll make you a wonderful wife." Then he added gruffly, "Come on, get busy! We're going to finish this job before dark. Don't even think about leaving early!" He laughed again and we went back to work.

I tried to keep my mind on the work, but I was brooding over Mary's response. What had caused that look on her face? Something was different. Something had happened. I expected her to be the same bubbly, open person she always was, like when she greeted James. I expected her to be just as excited to see me, even more so. But that strange look in her eyes...I didn't understand.

As soon as we finished, I jumped down saying, "I'll get my tools tomorrow." Normally, I stayed for the evening meal with James and his family. But not this time! As I was leaving, I heard James saying, half under his breath, "You don't have to be in such a hurry! She'll wait for you!" He kept talking, but I didn't wait to hear what he was saying.

After a quick cleanup I was on the way to Mary's home. If anyone had been watching me closely, they might have thought I was drunk. I started out walking fast, hurrying to see Mary after all this time. Then, remembering the look on her face, I slowed down. *But, she's back; everything must be okay.* My pace quickened until another thought surfaced. *Why that look, what made her look away from me?* My churning thoughts and uneven gait more than doubled the time it normally took to get to her house.

When I arrived, I was greeted cordially by her parents, but cooly by Mary. It was that way all evening. Mary talked excitedly about cousin Elizabeth, how she was going to have a baby, how they had given up hope of having children till now. How Zechariah had some illness and couldn't talk. But she said nothing about herself. Every time I looked at her—no, I was watching her all the time—every time she looked up at me, she looked away quickly. I could tell something strange was going on. She couldn't look me in the eye. Something was troubling her. Perhaps she had something to tell me, but just couldn't find the words. I'm sure my frustration showed as well. It was so strange! I said earlier when I saw her on the road she looked like she had been caught stealing dates. That's true, but there seemed to be no shame in her eyes, only mystery. And that was even more puzzling. Finally, I had to say good night and leave. As I started down the lane, I heard her Mother say, "Mary, you must be very tired or sick. I've never seen you treat Joseph the way you did tonight."

"I know, Mother, I'm..." Oh, how I wanted to stop, turn around and listen to the rest of that conversation, but I couldn't.

———————

Even before our betrothal, Mary and I had an unusual relationship. I had known her for almost a year before we were pledged to each other. I had become friends with her parents through some work I had done for them. From the beginning, their payment was more than just a chicken or produce. It was a well prepared meal and fellowship afterwards. The first time I went to their house for a meal, I remember that Mary listened intently to our conversation. Of course she never joined in, but it seemed she was always close by.

I often asked her father what we could do about the political situation. "Why are we still subjects of Rome?" I would cry. "Why do God's promises never come true?" Mary's father always steered me back to the Scriptures saying, "Be patient, Joseph. God works in His own time."

Gradually, my visits became regular—whether I'd worked for them or not. As time went by Mary would sometimes join us and listen. Before long, she began to ask questions or make comments of her own which were usually exactly on target. I admired her spunk and boldness, something I was a little short of.

I also dined with other families from time to time. Some had daughters who were at the age to be pledged or betrothed, but most of them seemed frivolous, stuck on themselves, or overly concerned about their appearance. It wasn't just the daughters. The fathers were uninterested in the subjects I wanted to talk about. All they wanted to discuss was money and how to get more. Usually, I left as soon as politely possible.

At Mary's home I felt comfortable, almost like a member of the family. Of course much of that feeling had to do with Mary.

One evening after a delicious meal, I suggested to Mary's father that we go out for a walk. I think he knew what was on my mind. As we walked, he waited patiently. He was used to my silences. Finally, on our way back to the house, he asked, "Joseph, was there something you wanted to ask me?"

Even with that open invitation, I still hesitated. "Well, you know I don't have much.... I'm just a poor carpenter..."

He stopped me. Putting his hand on my shoulder, he looked me full in the face and said with a curious smile, "Joseph, just ask."

Still, I hesitated. I knew I didn't deserve Mary—knew that I had almost nothing to give her. But compared to anyone else—there was simply no one like Mary! Finally, through chattering teeth and with clenched fists, I forced the words out, "Sir, I'd like to be pledged to your daughter, Mary." I nodded my head as if to say, now you have it!

"Joseph, Joseph, we knew this was coming! You'll never guess how many times her mother and I have talked about it."

My heart fell. I was convinced he was going to say that they had planned long ago how to say no to me.

But he continued, "Nothing would give us more pleasure than to see you and Mary pledged. Frankly, it would keep others from badgering me about their sons being pledged to her. But..."

I knew it! He was finally getting to the part about why I wasn't suitable! With my fists still clenched, I listened as he continued.

"But Mary is a little too young, in my opinion, to actually become betrothed. I realize that some of our people marry off their daughters as early as possible. However, her mother and I feel that it would be better to wait at least another year until the betrothal. Then naturally there will be another year before she is completely your wife."

Wife? Did he say, your wife? I must be dreaming, I thought.

He brought me back to earth as he shook me and said, "Joseph, are you okay?"

"Yes, I, ah, ah, I, I expected you to say no."

"Well," he said with a twinkle in his eyes, "what do you have for a dowry—to pay me for my loss?"

Oh no! I knew there was something I had forgotten! Of course I knew about the bride-price, but this was usually the groom's father's task. I had simply overlooked it in my fear of being rejected.

"Sir, I have nothing...nothing, I'm afraid...." I said, my voice trailing off in dismay.

"Joseph, I'm sure you have something to pledge. What do you have?"

Thinking furiously, *what do I have? What do I have?* I finally said, "I have a very small carpentry business, but that's about all. I will gladly pledge that, if it's acceptable."

"Oh Joseph, you have much more than that," he replied.

Puzzled, I looked at him. I had nothing, nothing at all. Was he just teasing me?

Looking stern, yet loving he said, "What about your character, Joseph? You are honest. You have a loving heart, and a heart that is quick to trust. I like that. Would you be willing to pledge your character?"

Overjoyed that he spoke so highly of me, I replied, "Sir, I pledge everything that I have and everything I am!"

"Then that is enough. I am happy and I'm sure Mary and her mother will be happy as well." We shook hands on this very unusual marriage proposal. Then he said, "Perhaps, you should go to your house now, while I break the news to Mary and her mother." I walked home on air!

After the pledging, I spent even more time at Mary's home. After meals—always with her parents present—Mary and I talked at great length about our lives, our country, our plans, about our deep love for God. I knew her feelings, her beliefs, and her hopes. I thought I knew everything about Mary.

I trudged home slowly after I left Mary's house on the night of her return from Elizabeth's. Troubled in heart, I mulled over what had happened that evening. Nothing made sense! Everything was confusing! But something kept fluttering through my mind—something I couldn't put my finger on. Slowly, it surfaced to my consciousness. When Mary was talking about Elizabeth's pregnancy she rubbed her stomach as if there was some connection between the two. *What could that possibly mean?* I immediately put the idea out of my mind. Keeping it out, though, was impossible—it kept returning. Then it gradually, dawned on me that Mary might be with child. What a repugnant idea! Impossible! Every time the thought surfaced, I rejected it.

Mary—pregnant? NO! That was simply impossible! Some other girl maybe, but not my Mary. But try as I could to stifle it, the idea kept growing.

The more I thought about it, the more possible it seemed. On the other hand, if she had told me face to face, I wouldn't have believed her. But however I looked at it, nothing else seemed to fit. When I finally accepted the idea that she perhaps was pregnant, I was shaken to the core. "If this is true," I whispered, "I only thought I knew her."

I needed to know, now, what had really happened! My mind raced. *Is that why she was gone for three months? Who is responsible for this? It couldn't be Mary's fault!* Anger, frustration, resentment, fear and yet love swept over me, wave after wave, back and forth.

To add to my dilemma, I began to wonder how I could tell Mary about my suspicions. I didn't want to accuse her—I knew in my heart she wasn't guilty of whatever had happened. But why should I have to say anything? Wasn't it her place to tell me? She loved God as much as I did. Why couldn't she tell me instead of me having to confront her?

The worst part of it all was the confusion. On one hand, I still loved Mary—deeply—regardless of what might have happened. And I thought she still loved me. On the other hand, I was angry. If Mary was pregnant, why didn't she tell me?

I wandered into my shop and lit a couple of lamps, seeking solace among the tools and wood I loved. Normally, as I rubbed my hand over the grain of the wood, I felt an affinity with it. That night I only felt hardness and coarseness. In anger and disgust I threw one piece across the room and almost broke a lamp. "Yiiiii!" I cried as I realized how close I came to starting a fire and burning down my shop. As hard as I tried, there was no solace in the wood or the tools.

In my dejection, self-doubt crept in. I certainly was not the dashing sort of man most girls wanted to marry. I almost always felt out of sorts with my thin lanky body, like the joints in my legs and arms never quite cooperated. My hair and beard were as unruly as they come. No wonder Mary...yet, I'd never seen any of these deficiencies reflected in her eyes. I could only assume she loved me.

Then an even greater dilemma dawned. Not only could I think of no way to confront Mary, I realized I couldn't say anything about Mary's situation to anyone else! I couldn't even ask for advice. If Mary's condition was known, I wouldn't be able to protect her. One purpose of the betrothal is to prove that the bride is a virgin. The law was clear: a betrothed woman who became pregnant was to be stoned to death. I couldn't allow that. In spite of my confusion and my aching heart, I was still committed to Mary. I loved her. But what could I do?

My problem seemed unsolvable. Even though I loved her, how could I marry her and assume that nothing had happened? The only solution I could think of was to divorce her. It would have to be done quietly—perhaps I could just send her away and no one would notice. Not likely! Was it even possible to 'divorce quietly?' I didn't know. But even if it was, it wasn't good. Not good for me...I wanted to be with her, love her, protect her. And it wasn't good for Mary either. No doubt she would be ostracized by the community. But a discreet divorce was the only possibility I saw. If word got out that she had 'played the harlot' and I married her anyway, it would kill my business. The few regular customers I had would leave me. But that was the least of my worries. Poverty I could live with! But how could I live with Mary—now—if this were true? And how could I live without her?

That night, with these thoughts tumbling through my head, was like...how can I express it? For a Jew it was like sitting in a pig sty. I was utterly miserable, sick to my stomach. I couldn't sleep. I couldn't think clearly. How could I face anyone? I rehashed my decision to divorce her. People would find out and start to talk regardless of how quiet we tried to keep it. I wondered about Mary. How could she have disgraced me this way?

As I tossed and turned on my bed, I vacillated between anger at what I thought might have happened, and a desire to protect Mary. I thought of how I had learned to love her and had waited for her. I thought of the little gifts I had given her as an expression of my love. I remembered the ecstasy of giving her the cradle and the look of love and trust she had expressed on receiving it. And all our talks about God—how she had learned from her mother and father to love and trust God for everything. And now this!

I curled up on my bed, my knees to my chest and cried. As I cried, I prayed passionately, "Oh God, please don't let this be true!"

30

4

The Water Bucket

What's that? In the midst of my tossing and turning I suddenly sensed someone or something in my room. Startled, I sat up. Someone stood at the foot of my bed! It looked like a man, but he was glowing and looking straight at me. I shrank away from him, my knees touching my chest as I cowered under my blanket. After what seemed an eternity, he spoke reassuringly and slowly:

Joseph, son of David, do not be afraid to take Mary as your wife. For the child within her was conceived by the

Holy Spirit. And she will have a son, and you are to name him Jesus, for he will save his people from their sins.[1]

Before I could say a word, he—or it—disappeared. I straightened up, wide awake. *What had he said? Mary was pregnant by the Holy Spirit? What does that mean? A son will be born and I'm to call him Jesus? Savior?*

The more I thought about the message, the less I understood it. After a few moments, I seemed to recall something from the Scripture that talked about this, but I couldn't remember it all. I was too tired, my mind too erratic to think clearly. Finally, I was able to focus on one thought—if this was true, it was the solution to my dilemma!

So this was the reason for the strange look in Mary's eyes—the reason she didn't tell me? She really is pregnant and...and it's okay? No wonder she didn't know how to tell me. She wouldn't expect me to believe a story like that. But is it really true?

As I mulled over the angel's words—for I was pretty sure it had been an angel—my spirit began to calm. Gradually, a prophecy from the Scriptures that I'd heard many times

---

1. Matthew 1:20-21

began to surface. *A virgin will have a child...they will call him Immanuel... 'God with us.'* Could this be true?

Well, yes, it was certainly true—it was in the Holy Scriptures! But is this—the events happening right now, to Mary, to me—a fulfillment of that prophecy? I could hardly believe it. And yet, gradually it began to sink in. As it did, I looked up to heaven and said softly, "Glory! Hallelujah!" With that I fell back in bed exhausted, but relieved, and was soon sound asleep.

I awoke before dawn the next morning, as I usually did. My first thought was, *What a strange dream I had!* Shaking my head, I sat straight up and said out loud, "That wasn't a dream!"

For the next few moments I rehearsed everything that happened the night before. First I thought of the angel and what he had said. The fantastic part was not so much that an angel had visited, as unusual as that was, but that an angel had visited me! Who was I? Sure, I was a descendant of King David, but so what? I tried to make sense of it and the angel's message, but I couldn't complete one thought—my mind was racing.

There were chores to be done, but that was the last thing on my mind that morning. I would start one job, lose interest and move onto something else. I was impatient to run to

Mary's house and tell her what had happened, but it was simply too early. I began to wonder if the sun would ever rise!

As I waited, I thought of what I would say when we met. There was no need to confront her now, but how could I tell her that an angel had visited me? Would she believe me? Was it really an angel? Doubts began to creep in. All I knew for sure was that someone had given me a message that this baby was from God—that I should go ahead and take Mary as my wife. I didn't understand it all, but it solved a huge problem for me; the confusion of my soul was lifted.

I could wait no longer. The carpentry could! It was still early morning when I set out toward Mary's house. As I walked, I whistled an old song from the Chronicles of the Kings:

Give thanks to the Lord and proclaim His greatness.

Let the whole world know what He has done.[2]

When I turned the corner onto Mary's street, there she was, coming my way carrying a water bucket. She was walking slowly, her shoulders slumped, her head hanging down. She didn't see me. I started to call out to her, then stopped abruptly. *She must be sorrowing over me,* I thought. *She must have guessed that I know something is wrong! Could*

---

[2] I Chronicles 16:8

she think I mean to harm her, to follow the letter of the law? Oh, how my heart went out to her. She looked so alone, so dejected. I walked slowly toward her, watching her, loving her, waiting until we were close before I spoke. I wanted her to be able to look into my eyes and know immediately how I felt.

She continued to look down. When we were just a few steps from each other, she finally heard my footsteps and started to look up. At that same moment, I said as compassionately as I could, "Mary!" Her head jerked up, first in fear, then in relief as she saw the smile and compassion I tried to convey through an unruly beard.

What a reunion that was—right there on the street! I knew it was not considered proper for a betrothed couple to be together like this, but I was too excited to care. Both of us began to talk at once.

"Oh, Joseph, I wanted to..."

"Mary, I just couldn't wait..."

We both stopped talking. She dropped the bucket and grabbed my hands, just for a second, then we stepped apart. She looked around for the bucket as I burst out, "You'll never believe who visited me last night." When she found the bucket, she stood up and looked quizzically at me, holding the bucket between us.

She looked so beautiful it was difficult to talk, but I did. "It is so wonderful to see you this morning, especially after last night."

"Yes, last night...I had so much I wanted to tell you, but I just couldn't find the words. I was so afraid, and still am, that you cannot or maybe will not believe what has happened." She paused for a moment, then added, "What did you say...about a visitor?"

"Believe it or not an angel visited me last night and... Ouch, that hurt!"

Picking up the heavy wooden bucket that had just landed on my toes, she said, "What did you say?"

"I said, that hurt. Sandals don't offer much protection."

"No, no, no. Your visitor?"

"Oh, that...I said it was an angel," I repeated, smiling proudly.

"An angel visited you, too?" She twisted around looking for the bucket again and added, "Come on! Let's go to my house and tell my parents." And she picked up the bucket and took off.

"Hey! Hold up a minute. My toe hurts! By the way, why do you have that bucket anyway?"

"Oh, yes, the bucket...I left the house this morning on the pretense of getting water, but knew I needed to see you, so..."

If someone was watching, what a scene they witnessed! Every few seconds the bucket fell to the ground and the one not talking would pick it up. Each of us was so full of our own story it was difficult to listen to the other's.

Mary told me she felt she had betrayed me. She regretted not telling me what had happened to her as soon as she got back from visiting Elizabeth. And I told her about the angel's visit and the joyful, yet mysterious message he gave me. It was a wonderful time! Neither of us understood the significance of these happenings or how difficult our lives would become. But in that moment there was a bond of oneness between us as we realized that God had spoken to both of us. There were no doubts now.

Our joy was inexpressible! Not only had Mary's parents chosen for us to be married, God, Himself had! After all the pain and anguish of the last day and night, I could hardly believe the joy of today. It was heavenly!

We were to have a baby boy and his name would be Jesus! "He would save his people from their sin," is what the angel had said. The Lord knew mankind needed saving! There were certainly a lot of 'sinners' in our country, and I wasn't thinking only of the Romans.

As we walked together to her house the bucket was between us, but our hearts were one. Our thoughts were jumbled as we walked—*What did all this mean? What should we do? How should we act? Do we tell people about this? If so, how? Even if we got married today how would we explain a baby that is born three months early?*

We had the answer to 'Should we get married?'—the angel gave us that one. But there were so many questions unanswered!

The day before, my vision of Mary had become tarnished and unlovely. Now, today, after the message from God, I looked at her with new eyes. How like that angel she was! Bright, shining, virtuous and a vessel used by God!

I particularly treasure something Mary said on that walk. "Well, since we are going to have a baby, at least we're prepared!"

"What do you mean?" I asked.

"The beautiful cradle you made, Joseph. It will be perfect for the Son of God!" Now, that was a proud moment for me.

By the time we reached Mary's home, we had decided one thing for sure—we should be married as soon as possible. But it had only been three months since our betrothal. We needed a good reason to break with tradition—otherwise, there would be unreasonable gossip in the community. Fortunately, we didn't need to worry. Mary's father gave us that 'good reason.'

5

The Reason

Nazareth, the place I called home, was an obscure village in Galilee. When Nazarenes traveled to Jerusalem, we faced the sneers of people who thought of us as simple, unsophisticated country people. Religious Jews also looked on us with disdain. Since Galilee shared borders with Gentile nations and strict Jews were deeply prejudiced against the Gentiles, they considered anyone or anything touched by a Gentile as unclean. The fact that Israel was ruled and scorned by conquering Gentiles didn't help.

Certainly we Galileans lived a much quieter life than Jerusalemites. Nestled among rolling hills, Galilee was a pastoral place which was perfect for those of us who preferred a simple life. However, it was not completely isolated. Some of the most traveled north/south and east/west trade routes ran close by our village. Fertile land surrounded Nazareth and, even though it was hilly country, the farming was good. The ancient olive trees almost produced on their own. But for me, the cool breezes and breathtaking views of the surrounding countryside more than made up for disparaging remarks I heard in the big city.

Living on the outskirts of Jewish country affected our education, as well. Not only did we speak a slightly different language from the well-educated Jerusalemites, we did not have the best religion teachers, either. At least that was the opinion of the higher class from Jerusalem.

There were many religious people in Nazareth in those days. Most of them dutifully attended synagogue and made the required sacrifices. Some gave to the poor and fasted regularly. And most kept the Sabbath, at least outwardly.

Mary's parents were different. They were authentic! They lived everything they professed, and they professed more than most. They were older—old enough to be my parents—and I looked up to them as if they were since my own had died many years before. Perhaps I felt a special closeness to them because they chose me to be Mary's husband. Yes, I'm sure that's true.

But I was not the only one who thought they were special. I never heard anyone speak about them except in the most reverent way, as if he was a godly priest and she was wisdom itself! It's no wonder they produced such a wonderful daughter!

———

When Mary and I arrived at her home with the empty water bucket, her mother was standing at the door, plate and dish towel in hand. "Looks like God worked out your problem?" she said, her face beaming as she flapped the dish towel at us. Her statement sounded like a question, but it was actually a command meaning, "Tell me all about it!" And this was good; she was a good listener—sympathetic and helpful. I was accustomed to it by now and would have felt slighted if she hadn't asked.

While Mary was sharing all about the visit of *my* angel, her father came in. He listened intently. I glanced at him from time to time, unsure of how much he knew of what had happened before today. When he didn't look too surprised, I relaxed a little. Still, I felt self-conscious being the center of attention.

When the story was finished, Mary's father hugged her and said, "Mother told me everything this morning after you left. I've been praying for you." Then he turned, looked me straight in the eye and spoke, haltingly, but with force: "Joseph, you're a blessed man! God is giving you a great honor. We've known about the prophecy of a virgin conceiving, but...our daughter? I'm...well, I'm overwhelmed. God bless you, Joseph! You're a man of faith...to believe Mary's story without question...to still accept her and take on...to still be willing to marry her and raise this child as your own...God bless you, Joseph!"

When he paused for a moment, I wanted to say, "I had a visit from an angel, too!" But he held up his hand to stop me, looked at Mother, then at his toes as he wiggled them in his sandals. He seemed to be gathering courage.

Shaking his head from side to side, he looked directly at me. "I'm afraid your faith will be tested many times in the days to come," he said. "I'm sure I don't understand everything I've heard, but ..." He looked down again, balled his hands into fists, then looking back at me, spoke confidently: "I still trust God!" With that he took a handkerchief out of his waistband, wiped his eyes and blew his nose. Then looking at each of us he said, "Now, what do we need to do?"

I was about to burst with excitement, apprehension, and joy—the moment was just too much! They must have felt the same way since no one was able to speak. Mary's father looked searchingly at us, waiting. Finally, coming to my senses, I broke the silence, "Well, we... uh, we've decided to get married[3] as soon as possible and..."

"Yes, I heard," he interrupted. "I'll take care of that. We can arrange it today. I know some friends will be upset with us breaking tradition, but we'll survive that storm." Then, as an afterthought he said, "By the way, did you hear about the census?"

"Caesar!" I grumbled, pounding my fist on the table. "I'll have to make a trip all the way to Bethlehem and be away from the carpentry shop for weeks, maybe more than a month!"

Isn't it funny how your emotions can change so quickly? Just the mention of anything connected with Caesar made me hopping mad! Impatient as ever, I was thinking, *Why doesn't God do something about the difficulties of His people?*

---

[3]Unlike our ceremonies, in marriage ceremonies of Joseph's day close friends and family gathered at the bride's home. The groom arrived, greeted everyone, received their blessings and then escorted his bride to his home.

Father countered softly, "What about Mary's condition? Does that affect your plans?"

Mary and I looked at each other, startled. We hadn't thought of that!

Her father went on, "Maybe to avoid wagging tongues, this would be a good chance to move to a new location...at least for the time being."

Mother was the first to catch what he was suggesting. "We hate for you to leave—now especially, but few people here would understand if you have a baby just six months after your wedding." This took a little time to sink in. Then she added, "We're willing to accept the censure of the public with you if—."

"Oh, Mother!" Mary interrupted with a little petulance.

"Wait a minute, suppose...maybe...just maybe that's the real reason for the census!" I chimed in. Things were beginning to make sense.

"What do you mean, the REAL reason?" Mary asked.

"Well, it suddenly struck me that you and I were visited by an angel...you're expecting a child, God's child and..."

"Yes, yes, I know...I believe that! But what does it have to do with the census?" Mary picked up a little of my impatience.

Ignoring her attitude, I went on. "Father, you know the Scriptures better than I do," I explained. "Isn't there something written about where Messiah is to be born?"

He answered quickly, "Yes, of course, one of the prophets said that Messiah will come out of Beth..." He stopped, looked at each of us and then said reverently, "Bethlehem."

"That's what I remember, too. So, as I said, perhaps this is the REAL reason for the census."

"Maybe so! Can you believe that God is even controlling what Caesar is doing?" Father exclaimed. "God is doing marvelous things!"

And I've been so impatient with God! I thought. *Perhaps God is doing something about the difficulties of the Jews after all.*

It was decided. If we had to go to Bethlehem sometime, it might as well be now. There was no sense in taking a chance on Mary's—or the baby's—health. As a matter of fact, we decided that the sooner we left, the better. There would be others returning to Bethlehem and if we got there before the crowd, perhaps we could find a decent place to stay. Maybe I could begin a carpentry business and we could live there for a while.

What tumultuous days! I was learning new things about the great God I love. I was learning that a man can trust God without knowing all the details or understanding everything. More than anything else, I knew...*we* knew that God was working in our lives.

Did I completely believe that the baby Mary was carrying was the Messiah? The best answer I can give is 'yes and no.' I knew in my heart that this was to be a very special birth, but I struggled with the fact that God would use *me*. He worked through great people, wealthy and successful people, didn't He? I was poor and unknown yet it seemed that God had chosen me. To think—*The angel called me by name!* In spite of my doubts, I determined to trust God completely and maybe just a little less impatiently.

6

The Journey

Our wedding took place that very evening—what a break with tradition! The small group of close friends who attended kept chattering among themselves. Only James, with his boisterous voice, was brave enough to ask what they were all wondering, "Why in the world are you rushing this?"

There was a whoosh as everyone took a deep breath, then dead silence. All eyes turned to me. I began hesitantly, "Well, I...uhm...Mary was away for a while and I have to go to Bethlehem for the census, you know that's where I was born...and...uh...I don't know how long that will be...we just don't want to be separated for a long time..." I finished feebly.

As I looked around I could see in their faces no one seemed to understand. Of course, I didn't tell them that Mary was already pregnant or that the baby she was carrying was the future Messiah. How could I? Although the census was a good reason for us to move away, it didn't make a lot of sense to those who didn't know the whole story.

Mary's mother brought some festivity back to the evening by announcing, "There's more food on the table, help yourselves!" There was flat bread to tear apart and dip in seasoned olive oil, fresh ripe dates, plump sweet figs and much more. I have no idea how Mary's mother put all that together, but it certainly helped.

So, we did honor tradition, only earlier than usual. And we were very glad that our family and close friends celebrated with us. Afterward, following tradition, I took Mary home to my little house for the first time.

We had planned to pack up our belongings and leave the following day, for I knew if we stayed, there would only be more questions. I hoped that the sooner we were out of sight, the sooner people would forget our breach of tradition.

The first night together in my humble little house/carpentry shop wasn't as I had often pictured my wedding night. In light of this special birth that was coming, we did not consummate our marriage. That would have to wait until sometime later.

Discussion of the trip to Bethlehem filled our evening and most of the night. What to take, what to leave, how to travel, when to travel, how to protect our precious cargo, etc. It became obvious that if I were to take the tools of my trade and set up shop in Bethlehem, I'd have to have some way to carry them. There was no furniture worth selling for I lived very simply. Work time was spent building for others. I had planned to cut back a little after our betrothal and begin to feather our future nest, but because of Mary's absence and my resulting doubts, I had not.

The only sellable thing we owned was the cradle. There was no way I could carry it and my tools. And too, I didn't want Mary to have to walk the whole distance. So we needed a donkey. When I first mentioned the idea of trading the cradle for a donkey Mary, with her hands on her hips, said, "No!" like she wasn't willing to discuss it. In the end, however, as much as we wanted to keep the cradle, we couldn't.

For this transaction, I thought of my best friend James. Actually, he was much more than a friend. He was more like a brother to me. Years ago, when I moved to Nazareth, he introduced me into the community. He pushed me to interact with people when I just wanted to be alone. When my faith faltered, James was there with a listening ear. He was the encourager I needed, since I had no family left to help me.

A few years younger than I, James was already married when we met. That was when he hired me to do some repairs on his house. After that first job, his home became my oasis. I had told James about the cradle and the careful work that had gone into it. He told me that if I ever wanted to sell it, he'd buy it sight unseen. However, when I approached him about it the morning after our wedding and told him that we were moving to Bethlehem immediately, he couldn't believe it.

"Hey, brother, I still cannot understand why the hurry. There's plenty of time! You don't have to go now for the census," he said. I just shook my head. I couldn't even tell my best friend, the reason for our haste! He knew I was hiding something, but didn't press me. Still, he looked hurt.

Nevertheless, James finally agreed to a trade...a donkey for the cradle. But when I showed him the cradle he said, "Joseph, that's a beauty! I tell you what, I'll give you two or three donkeys if you want them, Wow, I can't believe you would get rid of this!"

While I hesitated, not knowing what to say, he jumped in again, "Well, so is it two or three donkeys?"

"I really can't afford to keep more than one donkey," I protested, "and that's all we will need." Actually, hearing how much he liked the cradle, I hoped he would throw in a few pieces of gold, but I didn't want to ask.

Shaking his head he said, "I'll never understand you, Joseph. Running off like this in such a hurry, not asking a fair price. Oh, well..." and he went to get the donkey.

I had never owned a donkey. Even with the few things Mary and I owned, I needed James' help to pack everything on its back and tie it in place. As we worked, he said, "Now, Joseph, I want you to know this is the best donkey I have. He is the smartest, too. He's the very best." He was as proud of his donkey as I was of the cradle! James was tying the last knot on the load when he added, "Give this donkey a name—make him part of the family. If you take good care of him, he'll serve you well for a long time." Then he grabbed my shoulders, looked directly into my eyes and in a thick voice said, "You're a good man, Joseph, I'm going to miss you around here." Then as he hugged me, he added, "Name your first son after me!"

Mary and I said our goodbyes—shaking hands, giving kisses, receiving blessings—and among many tears, started on a journey we'd made many times, but never together. As I looked back at the little group of family and friends, I wondered if anyone noticed the twinkle in Mary's parents' eyes. Probably not. But anyone looking closely would have guessed that they knew something no one else in the group knew. Maybe it was the sparkle of grandmother and grandfather eyes. Perhaps it was the knowledge that Mary was carrying the Son of God in her womb. I hoped they would be able to keep the secret to themselves. There was an unspeakable joy and a bond between us because of our shared knowledge. It was going to be difficult, to say the least, to be separated from Mary's mother and father. There would be no one who knew our situation, no one with whom we could speak freely.

As we began our journey, I said, "I'm sure glad we don't have that old wooden bucket keeping us apart. My toes are still sore."

"I'm truly sorry about that, Joseph. Did we pack the bucket?"

"Yes, I filled it up with tools and tied it on somewhere."

As we walked, we talked about the people we'd left behind. Mary spoke lovingly of her parents and I 'amened' everything she said. Then she mentioned, "You're going to miss James, aren't you?"

"Yes, I am. He's been more than a best friend, even if he is a great teaser!" Pausing for a moment thinking about my last talk with James, "I think he guessed we were hiding something. He seemed hurt that I couldn't share it with him. I feel like a failure as a friend for not being open and honest with him."

A little later, I stopped and said, "Do you want to ride for awhile, Mary? That's one reason we got the donkey."

"Yes, it would be nice," she answered immediately, making me realize I should have asked sooner.

After rearranging the load a bit, I helped Mary onto the donkey and we continued our journey. Thinking about James and the donkey, I remembered, "Oh, by the way, James said we should give our new donkey a name. Got any ideas?"

Mary laughed, "What about naming him James?"

I frowned, "No, I think not. He asked me to name my first son after him and I wouldn't want a son and a donkey named James. Actually, I was trying to think of something from the Scriptures that might be significant."

"Okay. Something significant...well, what about 'Ballam'? His donkey talked!"

"That's true...and significant, but...I don't think I want to use that name. I mean, what if we had to get up in the middle of the night and call him? People would think I was crazy!"

"Okay let's see...if you needed to travel in the middle of the night, you would probably want to travel fast...what about 'Jehu?' Remember, 'he drove furiously.' "

"Jehu, hmmmm, I suppose if you're determined to give him a funny name, Jehu will do." Then I leaned over and spoke into the donkey's ear, "Is Jehu okay with you?" At that Jehu shook his head up and down, and we laughed for the first time that day. Before we knew it, darkness was coming. We found a place to stop and bedded down—our first night on the road.

The next morning we got up early, ready to start our journey at any moment. Thieves were common, so people normally traveled in large groups for protection. That's how we always traveled to Jerusalem for the Feast of the Passover. A big party all the way. But on this trip, I wanted to be alone with Mary. My plan was to watch the other groups traveling and when an honest looking bunch gathered to leave, get on the road just before them. We did this most of the trip, trying to stay about 100 cubits ahead of the group. When the road became rough or there were many curves, we slowed down and tried to stay in sight. I hoped that any thieves, who spotted us, would soon see the others and leave us alone.

Relatively alone then, Mary and I had the time and freedom to talk over the events that had happened and catch up on each other's stories. On the second day I decided to learn more about hers. Not knowing how she would respond, I ventured, "We've talked so much about what the angel said to me, I've been wondering what he said to you. You don't have to tell me..."

"Oh, Joseph, I want to!" She spoke excitedly, "Things have been happening so fast, I can't really think straight. As a matter of fact I was just going over in my mind what he said because I don't want to forget it. I'll start at the beginning...the evening you gave me the cradle. I was so happy I couldn't get to sleep. Then without any noise or movement this person appeared in the room and said, 'Greetings, favored woman! The Lord is with you!'[4]

I didn't know what to think! But the angel went on,

Don't be afraid, Mary, for you have found favor with God! You will conceive and give birth to a son, and you will name him Jesus. He will be very great and will be called the Son of the Most High. And the Lord God will give him the throne of his ancestor David. And he will reign over Israel forever; his Kingdom will never end![5]

---

[4]Luke 1:28

[5]Luke 1:30-33

"Now, for sure, I didn't know what to think!" she continued. "We had just that day become engaged, but the angel didn't mention you. He said that I would conceive and give birth to a son. So I asked, 'But how can this happen? I am a virgin.' "[6]

I interrupted her, "That's what I want to know!"

"The angel told me, 'The Holy Spirit will come upon you, and the power of the Most High will overshadow you. So the baby to be born will be holy, and he will be called the Son of God.' "[7]

"Then he added something to help me believe that the impossible would happen...,

What's more, your relative Elizabeth has become pregnant in her old age! People used to say she was barren, but she's now in her sixth month. For nothing is impossible with God."[8]

Mary paused. After a minute of contemplation, I said, "If I didn't know better, I'd say it was impossible!" Then asked, "Is that all?"

---

[6]Luke 1:34

[7]Luke 1:35

[8]Luke 1:35-37

"No, I'm just thinking back...I made a commitment to God at that point and said to the angel,

I am the Lord's servant. May everything you have said about me come true.[9]

Then the angel left."

We were quiet for a while as we reveled in the sunshine of God's grace and love. After a while I commented, "It really hurt me when you left to go visit Elizabeth without even saying...something."

She put her hand on my arm, "I'm so sorry, Joseph, but I needed some time to sort all these things out. I thought if Elizabeth was experiencing such a great miracle, perhaps she could help me with mine. I didn't even tell my parents about the angel or the news about Elizabeth either!"

"I've been wondering when you would tell me about your unplanned visit." I would have added, *and that almost wrecked me*, but stopped in time and kicked a stone in the middle of the road.

"Oh, Joseph, it was simply wonderful! I hope you get to meet Elizabeth and Zechariah sometime. They have such great faith and trust. Elizabeth said the most amazing thing when she greeted me, 'Blessed are you among women, and

---

[9]Luke 1:38

blessed is the child you will bear!' Then Elizabeth told me that when she heard my voice her baby leaped in her womb. What a comfort and blessing that was. She already knew!"

All I could say was, "Wow!"

After a few meditative moments watching the dust from the road curl up around our feet I added, "You mentioned the other night that Zachariah had some kind of illness and couldn't talk. What happened to him?"

"No one seemed to know." She tugged playfully at my arm, "Besides it was a little difficult to find out from him since he couldn't talk!"

"If he could, you ladies probably wouldn't have given him a chance!" I laughed, but when I looked up at Mary, she was frowning and plucking the petals from a flower I had picked for her earlier.

As she pulled off the last petal, she smiled and said, "You may be right because if he could have talked, we wouldn't have asked him why he couldn't talk, would we?" We both chuckled at that.

Mary went on to tell me about her time with Elizabeth and Zechariah. I determined that if we had the chance, we would visit them one of these days. They lived close to Jerusalem, so perhaps...

There was a pause in our conversation as we walked and silently meditated on these things. Then, without warning, Mary began singing the song the Lord inspired in her. I can only remember the first few lines...

Oh, how I praise the Lord.

How I rejoice in God my Savior!

For he took notice of his lowly servant girl,

and now generation after generation

will call me blessed.

For he, the Mighty One, is holy,

and he has done great things for me.[10]

Day after day we traveled on. We spent the time pondering the preceding events and wondering what this little son that was to be born into our family would be like. We didn't talk much about who this son was. Perhaps it was just too sacred, too wonderful, or perhaps it was simply that we didn't fully understand. Something we did discuss was 'what if?' What if one of us had said 'no' to the angel? We never came up with an answer, and we never again talked about it after the trip to Bethlehem.

During these days on the road our love deepened as we grew to know each other better. Even though we freely

---

[10]Luke 1:46-49

expressed our love for each other, I still found it hard to believe that Mary could love me. What did I have to offer her? I was so poor that everything I had could be put on the back of a donkey with room left for her to ride! But one thing I did have—something that most mothers wanted for their daughters—a good lineage. I was a descendant of King David. You couldn't come from a better family than that! On the practical side, though, it never put a chicken in the pot for supper. That Mary loved me was never a question. I just never quite understood why.

The six days of travel were six days of release. Once we left Nazareth, we were able to slow down...come down to earth. A dusty earth in our case! We had experienced so many pivotal events in the last few months, we needed this time. God had given me a new job as protector—protecting Mary from the accusing voices of society and providing a protected place, a home for the little miracle son that was to be born. I was also learning more about love—that love is commitment. I could not love Mary without being committed to her, nor could I love God without commitment to Him and His will.

The closer we got to Bethlehem, the more people we saw on the road. It seemed that others had the same idea we did—get there early to find a place. None of us returning Bethlehemites knew for sure what day the census officials would be in town. And once they appeared the process could take days. Furthermore, if the officials called for your family and you weren't there to be counted, you could be put in jail when they caught up with you.

Another problem was space. Bethlehem wasn't exactly a big city! Since it was on one of the trade routes, there was a constant flow of visitors who stayed for a day or two. But even for the tradespeople, there were very few inns. That meant two things. First, it would probably be difficult for us to find a place to live and, secondly, there might not be work for me.

7

Bethlehem

Our last night on the road was spent in Jerusalem. We planned it that way. Since we had traveled there every year for Passover, there were several inns where we could stay without questions being asked. We would just be two of the many travelers on the road. Another advantage was that it gave us a short trip on the last day of our journey. Since we needed to find a place to live, I figured we would get there in plenty of time to look around, find something, and settle our few things before nightfall.

The surprise of that last day came early, just after daybreak. We had taken to the road expecting, hoping to have it to ourselves. Unfortunately, several other families had the same idea. There were four, or perhaps five groups already on the road. Unlike us, most were traveling light. I hoped they were traveling past Bethlehem.

About midmorning, we met another family coming toward Jerusalem. They seemed a friendly bunch. As we met, the man greeted us and asked where we were headed. I told him and he frowned. I stopped. "What's wrong with Bethlehem?"

"Nothing's wrong with Bethlehem, it's just that there's no place for a family to live. We spent the last week trying to find a place and nothing's available."

Fishing for more information I asked, "Why did you want to settle in Bethlehem?"

"Well, my trading business causes me to travel a lot and I need to be some place close to Jerusalem. But, I'm not particularly fond of big cities, especially since I travel and have to leave my family. What about you? Why are you going to Bethlehem?"

That jolted me! *Do I tell him an angel appeared to me and told me...or that my wife is going to have a baby that's not mine, but rather God's?* It's funny how quickly thoughts like these can run through your mind. I answered, "Well, my wife's expecting a baby and with the census coming up, we decided it would be better to go now. We hope to find a place to live and set up my carpentry business. It *is* my family home so we'd have to make the trip sometime."

He frowned, "Why didn't you just make the trip by yourself? You don't have to have your family with you!"

"I realize that, but you see, we've just been married a short time and I don't think I could leave my wife, even for a few days. And too, our home was in Nazareth," I added.

"That is a long trip to make," he exclaimed, "especially when you're not sure when the census takers will actually be in Bethlehem." Then leaning closer he added under his breath, "Of course, when you have five kids like me, you might enjoy a trip like this alone!"

"So you think we won't be able to find a house?"

"It'll be difficult. Of course, I wasn't looking for a small place, but I don't remember seeing anything that was available." He paused, then added, "There were a few places, but they were being held for relatives who would be coming later. There will be plenty of places after the census. Maybe we'll be back then. I'll look you up. You're a carpenter? I could probably use a good carpenter. Well, we better get going.

Shalom, brother!" And with a wave of his hand and crack of the whip, he restarted his family's procession.

Mary and I looked at each other questioningly, wondering if we had made the right decision. After a moment, when neither of us spoke, we said hopefully, and almost in unison, "God will provide!"

As we resumed our journey, we thought seriously about the move we were making. This was not in the plan! Before, everything about going to Bethlehem was wonderful, glorious. But now?

When we finally arrived, I decided that the inn was the best place to begin our search. The innkeeper would probably know if there were any available places. If not, we could stay at the inn for a little while—a very little while, since we had already spent most of our money.

Like most innkeepers, he was rotund, jovial and busy. Before I could say anything, he said, "NO ROOM! No Room! No room! How many times have I had to say that? Sorry sir, there's simply no room in the inn."

I could tell he was frustrated. What innkeeper wouldn't be? He probably had only a few guests a week in normal times and now he could make a killing if he just had more rooms. That gave me a clue. "Yes, I'd heard that there was no place. I met a businessman on the way who told me. So, I wonder . . .

I'm a carpenter. Maybe I could build some new rooms for you."

"Great idea!" he bellowed, "But you'd probably stay just long enough to get something started, then the census would be over and you'd leave. Yes? Besides, I still don't have anywhere for you to stay."

"Actually, my wife and I were planning to move here. She's going to have a baby soon, so we really do need a place. And...I really am a good carpenter."

Hands on his hips, the innkeeper repeated, "Hey, I like the idea, I just don't have a room."

I looked back at Mary. She could hardly stand, she was so exhausted. Pleadingly, I turned to the innkeeper, "Sir, we've traveled all the way from Nazareth. There has to be some place—anyplace as long as there is some shelter."

"From Nazareth, hmm...anyplace? I wouldn't even offer this to a Samaritan, but it looks like you're desperate. Tell you what I'll do," he said in a loud whisper. "We have a stable out back and we only have one cow at the moment. You could clean up the stable and stay there. I won't charge you anything. But you'd have to do odd jobs and maybe some carpentry work. Heaven knows there's plenty to be done!"

"That sounds like a bargain to me, sir," I said with a sigh, "I knew God would provide a place."

He looked at me strangely, like he might change his mind. "You knew *what*?"

But I was already on my way out to tell Mary the good news. When no one else could find a place to stay, God held one open for us!

So we settled in the stable. Actually, there was plenty of room, even for Jehu. The back of the stable opened into a cave which was nice. Cool in the daytime and not too cold at night.

One of our great concerns was that someone would discover that Mary's pregnancy preceded our wedding. We kept trying to think of what to say if that happened. How could we excuse ourselves? People were generally not very forgiving and, if the story got around, no doubt we would be shunned. After all, that was why we left Nazareth so quickly. If someone asked, could we just tell them that this baby was the result of the Holy Spirit? Hardly! We'd have been laughed out of town. If someone knew Mary's parents, they might believe that, but no one else would.

We never came up with an answer—fortunately no one ever asked. That was one of the most amazing wonders of all. The normal questions asked any couple having their first baby, especially a new couple coming into a community, were simply never asked. Perhaps it was because the census provided so many other things to talk about. Maybe. But I never believed it. I knew God was at work! He was controlling the events, and Mary and I were clay in His hands. We were being molded and shaped and used—we hoped—for His glory. The census takers finally came. The process seemed to take forever. By the time it was over and the other census visitors had left, Mary was too far along for us to move to a more suitable place.

I get emotional just thinking about the events that followed. Almost too emotional to tell about them! Even now, after so many years, I'm in awe at what happened, how it happened, and how little we understood the importance of these events.

8

The Birth

With great excitement, we the made all the normal arrangements for having a baby. A midwife was found who agreed to help us, although she wasn't very happy about making a house-call in a stable. She was even less happy at the thought of a baby being born there. When she voiced this concern on her first visit, we assured her that a house would open up as soon as the census was over—that could happen any day, now—and we'd move to a more acceptable place.

But as time passed and Mary's due date came closer, we realized that the baby just might be born in the stable. Actually, it didn't bother us that much. We had gotten used to living there, and since Mary kept the place so clean, even the midwife accepted the fact that it really wasn't much different from a house. On the other hand, it was unusual. I'm sure the midwife got a lot of laughs when she told the story of the poor family in the stable who were going to birth a baby there.

One evening after supper, Mary was resting and I was cleaning up after our simple meal. We knew the baby was due any day, but when Mary suddenly cried out, "Joseph, it's time!" I froze. Then I remembered that I was supposed to go for the mid-wife. But before I could get to the door, Mary cried out again, "Joseph, I need you...NOW!"

I ran to her just in time to see the baby emerging. She told me what to do as if she did this every day. I was amazed! And all thumbs! I'm used to working with solid objects like wood and here was this little mass of flesh and bones who let out a cry like I'd pinched him or something! As soon as I could get the baby disentangled and the cord cut—according to Mary's instructions, of course—I handed him to her. He soon stopped crying.

As Mary cleaned him up and admired him, I admired her. *If having babies was no more trouble than this,* I thought, *we'd have a dozen or two!* Little did I realize that this birth was unusual. You might think I'm not too bright. There was a miraculous conception; there were angels delivering special messages—and I didn't realize that this would be an unusual birth? All I can say is that in the midst of the excitement, one tends to forget.

I was kept busy running back and forth getting things for Mary. She needed warm water. She needed a cloth. She needed...all sorts things! Of course, she had to tell me where everything was since I wasn't in the habit of working around the home. My carpentry work left me little extra time.

"Joseph, get the swaddling cloths for me to wrap baby Jesus." Her voice aroused me out of my reverie.

"Where are they?"

"I thought they were right there on the hay."

"I don't see them anywhere."

"Well, get something else. You can search for it later."

"Will this do?" I asked, holding up a clean tunic of mine.

"Sure, that's fine for now. But you need to rip it into strips so I can wrap him up good...and tight."

After I started ripping the cloth, I realized this was the tunic I'd wrapped the cradle in that special night that now seemed like years ago. Tears welled up in my eyes as I remembered all that had happened. Since we couldn't keep the cradle, I had saved the tunic as a memento. But I was already ripping it before I realized its significance. Tears in my eyes, I ripped away. I took the strips to Mary. As she wrapped them around the newborn baby, I asked, "Where are we going to lay him? We don't have a cradle. I'm sorry, I forgot to make another one."

"You didn't forget, Joseph. You've been working so hard you haven't had time," Mary said lovingly. "I thought about it and cleaned out the manger over there. It hasn't been used since we've been here. It'll work just fine."

Amazingly, God had provided his son with a cradle even though I hadn't been able to!

It's a lot of work having a baby, but finally, things quieted down. Rest at last! Though it was late and we were both tired, it was difficult to take our eyes off the little bundle of joy in Mary's arms. I wondered, *Is this really God's son?* He looked so...so normal. Looking at Mary, I knew she was doing the same—reviewing all that God had brought into our lives. How He brought us together, the angels' visits, the census. (Wouldn't Caesar be mad if he knew that God had used the census to create a cover for the birth of a King who would rule in his place?) Yes! This was certainly God's Son!

As we rested, my mind wandered. *What if everything had gone as planned and I'd called the midwife? Right now there might be scores of busybodies here. Undoubtedly, as soon at the midwife left—probably before—people would have started showing up, wanting to see the baby. Well, perhaps not scores, but at least two or three! This was OUR baby...almost. At least ours to protect; ours to feed; ours to train.* Suddenly, I sat up straight. *How do I train the son of God?*

Then I prayed, "Thank you, Lord, for the peace and quiet and for this son of ours...I mean, thank you for this son of yours." I paused for a moment, then added, "Help us to trust and believe you more—and depend on You for his training."

9

The Visitors

Baby Jesus was sleeping peacefully and Mary was resting. Just as I started to blow out the lamp and get some rest myself, the gate creaked. Then I heard whispering and excited voices coming to our door. Walking brusquely to the door, I cracked it open and whispered urgently, "We've got a new born baby in here!" *What in the world could shepherds want here at this time of the night?* It was easy to see and smell that they were shepherds. For a moment I thought they had brought the flock with them, but I didn't hear any bleating.

"Hey, fellows, this must be the place! They have a new born baby here!" one of them shouted.

"Shhh, not so loud!" I cautioned them. "What do you mean, this must be the place?"

"We were told there was a baby born in Bethlehem tonight."

"That's strange," I paused, thinking. "No one from town has been here and it just happened. Who told you?"

"Angels!" He said, grinning from ear to ear.

"Angels?" I questioned, a little more interested.

Looking over the group of shepherds, I could see them all nodding in agreement. It was clear they had all seen the angels and they weren't going to leave until they saw the baby.

"Just a minute!" I turned around to check on Mary and the baby. Instead of sleeping, Mary was sitting up in bed, hair combed and waiting.

"It looks like we have company," I growled.

"I heard. Be gracious, Joseph, we're fine."

I glanced quickly at Jesus, asleep in the manger. Then I looked back at Mary, marveling. *How could she look so beautiful this late at night and after just having a baby?*

Turning back to the entrance, I said, "Okay, gentlemen, come on in. See the baby for yourselves." I bowed and let them enter.

The shepherds were very quiet as they came in. They looked at Jesus, talking softly among themselves with little muttering sounds—sort of like sheep talking to each other. I had no idea what they were saying, but occasionally one of them would turn around and look at Mary or me then turn back to admiring little Jesus. Finally the young man, seemingly their spokesman, spoke up again.

"Well, mister, this is the baby the angels told us about!"

I responded incredulously, "Are you sure? How do you know?"

"As strange as it may seem, the angel told us we would find the baby wrapped in strips of cloth, lying in a manger. We all thought that was pretty strange, but when we came in and actually saw it, there was no doubting." He paused and then added, "By the way, why did you wrap him up with these torn strips? Don't you have regular swaddling bands?"

I answered rather stiffly, "Yes, we have everything we need, thank...!" My voice trailed off as I realized how rude I sounded. I continued apologetically, "It's just that, well, at the moment we needed them to wrap him I couldn't find them. So I ripped up one of my tunics. As a matter of fact," looking around the dimly lit cave-stable, "I still haven't found them."

"I'm sure my mom would lend you some. She just had a baby last month and we have more of those cloths than shepherd crooks!" he exclaimed proudly.

"Thank you." I tried to sound thankful, but I'm sure my voice was strained. "I imagine we'll find the bands in the morning light. By the way, what's your name?"

"Josiah." He paused, "Do you have a name for him yet? He's a beee-uuu-tii-full baby, as my Mother would say. Not like my baby brother...but don't tell Mom I said that!"

"Ok, I won't and his name is Jesus..."

"The angel said this baby is Christ the Lord. What does that mean?"

"I believe it means that He will be our Savior," I answered. "I was told He will save his people from their sins." I wanted to ask what else the angel told them, but they were focused on little Jesus. I didn't want to interrupt, so I quickly added, "Look, Josiah, why don't you come back in a few days and we'll talk about it?"

"You better believe I'll be back! And that's not all, we're going to tell everyone the good news we heard tonight and about all we've seen. You're going to have lots of visitors!" He turned back to look at the baby and probably would have stayed all night, if one of the older shepherds hadn't said, "We better go, guys, while we still have sheep to watch!"

"Do you mean that you left your sheep up on the hillside without someone to watch them?" I was amazed. Shepherds just don't do that!

Josiah looked at me like I was crazy, "Sir, an angel almost scared us out of our wits, then told us to not be afraid. He gave us the message about your son, then a choir showed up giving praise to God! Surely this was a message from God! Would you have stayed with the sheep?"

I had to admit that I would have done the same thing. I remembered how God had spoken to me through an angel in a dream. Yes, I would have definitely left the sheep.

The other shepherds were still admiring Jesus. One or two of them looked back at me and nodded in agreement with Josiah. After admiring the baby a bit longer, they picked up their crooks, stood up and bowed before Jesus. It was almost like they had rehearsed it. Then they turned to Mary, smiled sheepishly and gave her a little bow. One by one they shook my hand and went out in muffled silence.

As the gate creaked shut I heard their voices getting louder and louder. "Did you see that..." "I can't even believe my eyes!" "Just like the angel said!" "The strips of cloth..." Even after they returned to the hillside, I could still hear the buzz of excitement, although I could barely see them in the moonlight.

Now, I couldn't sleep! Mary and I had worshiped Jesus with the shepherds. They were so simple and trusting, just like the sheep they watched. We were both overcome with the excitement and wonder of that night. I gathered Mary into my arms, kissed her and, holding her hand, sat down on the bed beside her. It seemed like the first time we had sat quietly together meditating and talking since we arrived in Bethlehem. I commented on Josiah's remark about his mother having more swaddling bands than they had shepherd's crooks, and we both laughed.

We probably sat there for more than an hour just enjoying the quietness, occasionally commenting on the wonder of it all....just being together. Suddenly, Mary became restive. I started to get up, thinking it must be time to feed Jesus, but Mary grabbed my hand, brought it lovingly to her lips and kissed it.

"Joseph, do you remember on our trip to Bethlehem from Nazareth? There was one thing we disagreed on. Do you remember what it was?"

"Perhaps you should refresh my memory," I said, wondering what I'd done wrong.

"You were right!"

Now, I really wondered what she was talking about, but I held my tongue and waited.

"I always thought that we should tell people about Jesus, who he is and all that," she continued.

Now I remembered, but still kept quiet.

"You said to me very firmly, 'No, this is God's son. He will announce the coming of His son to whomever He pleases. It's not our responsibility!' Tonight I understand what you were saying."

I looked into her eyes and smiled. It wasn't often I got something like that right.

Mary responded mischievously, "You remembered that all the time and just waited for me to admit it, didn't you?"

"No," I paused, then added, "I'd actually forgotten. It's like you said earlier, I've been too busy to think about much of anything lately." Then a little disgusted, I said, "I still can't believe I forgot to make a cradle. Any carpenter can throw one together in a few minutes."

"Wait a minute, Joseph! What was it Josiah just told us about the angel's message?"

"I think he said, 'you will find the baby wrapped in strips of cloth.' "

"Ah ha! You missed part of it. He said, 'you will find the baby wrapped in strips of cloth, lying in a manger!' "

With that, my eyes filled with tears. God knew all along that Jesus would be in a manger! Overcome with wonder, Mary and I sang a duet of praise! Well, Mary actually did the singing. I just hummed along, saying, "Amen!" every now and then, thankful that God listens to the music of the heart, not necessarily that of the voice.

What a wondrous night that was! There we were, holding and admiring the Son of God! I was so thankful for the shepherds' visit—that angels visited them, too. When I finally got back to bed, I thought, *What a glorious day it will be on the morrow when the story gets out. When people hear that God's Son, the Redeemer, was born right here in Bethlehem!*

10

The Dedication

Josiah was as good as his promise. Almost too good! He showed up the next evening on his way to watch the sheep. Coming in quietly and respectfully, he knelt down next to the manger and looked lovingly at Jesus. Several times he reached out his hand to touch him, but didn't. I suppose he was afraid to wake him up. After a bit, he got up to leave.

When he got to the door, he looked at me with a twinkle in his eyes and said hopefully, "I wonder if we'll see angels tonight?" Then his face clouded over as he added, "We told everybody we saw about the message the angels gave us. And you know what? They just laughed at us! I could hear them saying under their beards, 'What do shepherds know?' as if we were stupid or something. When we told them that we actually came and found the baby just like the angels said, they said, 'So what! Lots of people wrap up a newborn baby like that!' Then I mentioned the manger," he continued sadly, "and again they just scoffed, 'If those folks are so poor they can't even afford a cradle, then a manger's good enough for them, IF IT'S CLEAN!' laughing like it probably wasn't. Was I ever mad!" With that and a shake of his head, he headed for the hills and the sheep.

The only other visitor we had that day was the midwife. She came in with a smirk on her face. You could tell she had heard the shepherd's story and didn't believe it, but she was polite. She checked to see that everything was okay, and shrugged her shoulders when Mary told her that she had no problems at all. "Well, that happens sometimes," she muttered. "Isn't usual, though!" When she put Jesus back in the manger, she looked at him for several minutes. I was sure that she would turn around and say something like, 'This is certainly an unusual and special son you have here!' Instead, she shook herself like she had dozed off for a moment and said, "Well, he looks normal to me. If you need anything, you know where to find me." And she left.

Mary and I were stunned. She spoke first, "Can you imagine, picking up, handling and admiring the Son of God and then only saying, 'He looks normal?'" Her voice trembled. She bit her lip, wanting to say more, but not daring to. As tears came to her eyes, I enfolded her in my arms, looked to heaven and prayed, "Oh mighty God, help us to be strong! Help us to trust you completely! Vindicate your mighty name! Oh, God, what will you have to do to redeem your people? Help us, Lord, it is so hard when we feel so alone. Help us trust you, Lord!"

As I was praying, Mary's arms went around me. They had been hanging limply by her sides, like she was completely drained. Now, she began squeezing me so tight I thought she might squeeze the air right out of my lungs. "Oh, Joseph, how I love you! You are so strong for me. Always comforting me, always loving me. God knew I needed someone just like you. Someone who is...mmm..."

"Stubborn?"

"Yes, as a matter of fact, stubbornly trusting in God. That's a wonderful trait, Joseph. Thank you!"

The next few days seemed to blend into one as things returned to normal. We didn't have all the visitors Josiah predicted. Perhaps it was because of the stories the shepherds told and people thought we might be strange. Perhaps it was because we were still in the stable—not everyone would want to call on poor strangers who lived in a barn! By the help of God, we were able to overlook the lack of visitors.

But Josiah came. Almost every day! Actually, he was a blessing. He was glad to get a bucket of water from the well or anything else that needed to be done. This was a big help to Mary since, after that first day, I had gone back to work. Most of my free time was now spent fixing up a small house that had been vacated after the taxation. It had been left in terrible shape—everything needed repairing. I worked hard. I wanted to move Mary and the baby out of the stable as soon as possible.

One evening, I came home a little earlier than usual. Josiah was still there. Mary had told me they often talked at length about Jesus and who he was. He was probably the only one in all of Bethlehem, besides Mary and me, who believed who Jesus was. I asked him something I had been wondering about.

"Josiah, remember the night you came to visit us with all the shepherds?" I said.

"Of course, it was only a few days ago!"

"Well...was this the first place you came to?"

"Sure was," he said like it was a stupid question.

"Umm. I've been wondering, how did you know to come here?"

"That wasn't difficult. The angel said that we would find the baby lying in a manger. Very few houses have mangers, you know, and then I knew that the couple living in this stable were expecting a baby. So I just put two and two together and brought all the other guys here."

"What about the angels? Were you afraid? What...?"

"You want to hear about the angels, don't you?" he laughed.

I nodded and waited. The angel visits to Mary and me were so central to who and where we were, we were extremely interested in hearing his story.

"Well, the first thing the angel said was, 'Don't be afraid!' And it's a good thing, too, because we were just about ready to run away and leave the sheep!" He paused, then went on, "What would you do if you saw a bright light and there was a person or something in it?"

Straightening his shoulders, Josiah said firmly, "I don't care how much the townspeople laugh at this story, this is exactly what the angel said,

'I bring you good news of great joy for everyone! The Savior—yes, the Messiah, the Lord—has been born tonight in Bethlehem, the city of David! And this is how you will recognize him: You will find a baby lying in a manger, wrapped snugly in strips of cloth!' "[11]

I sat there mulling this over, but especially the fact that the angel had told the shepherds about the strips of cloth.

Josiah woke me out of my reverie saying, "Well, I better go. Mom's not too happy I spend so much time here. I'm still trying to get her to come and see the baby for herself, but..."

"That's okay," I murmured, my hand on his shoulder, "God bless you, Josiah. And thanks for telling us what the angel said."

Mary did have one other visitor during those days in the stable. Josiah's mother finally came to see Jesus. She brought us some of the swaddling bands. "Josiah, said you might need these and we have more of these cloths than sheph...oh, Josiah told you that, too" she said, noticing that Mary was mouthing the words along with her.

When she saw Jesus she exclaimed, "He's a beee-uuu-tii-full baby!" exactly as Josiah thought she would. After she had visited a polite length of time and was ready to leave, she told Mary, "I know that Josiah spends a lot of time here. I've told him not to bother you..."

---

[11]Luke 2:10-12

"He doesn't bother us at all. Actually he's been a big help to me!" Mary assured her.

"He helps? He never does that at home. Oh, by the way, that story he keeps telling...I don't know what gets into shepherds' heads. I think spending all that time with sheep gives them wooly thoughts. Fortunately, my husband was able to move up to selling the sheep rather than just watching them. I had hoped that Josiah would follow him, but with all this talk about angels, well, it may be too late." And, with that, she was gone before Mary could reply. Once again, Mary felt rejected.

The next day we moved everything into the little house. Finally, a place we could call 'HOME!' A stable is okay if there's nothing else available, but it's not the type of place you want to call home. Best of all, Jesus had a new place to sleep—I had put together a simple cradle that, although not a work of art like my first one, could be moved around and used wherever we were. We were happy.

The eighth day of Jesus' life and the first morning in our new living quarters, we got up early and took him to the synagogue in Bethlehem to be circumcised. It was a beautiful morning, full of new hope and expectations. This was the first time Jesus would be out in public, the first visit to a priest. *Perhaps here he will be recognized for who he is! To be justified rather than vilified; to be looked up to rather than looked down on.* This was a precious thought.

When we met the priest, he casually asked, "What's the baby's name."

I responded proudly, "Jesus!"

The priest looked at us for a moment. I waited for him to recognize Jesus and say something about him being the Son of God. My excitement turned to dismay as a sly smile crept onto his face and he said, "Oh, then this is the baby the shepherds told that crazy story about. What will shepherds think of next?" As he spoke, I felt my face turning red as anger welled up inside me. I was just about to explode when Mary grabbed my hand and smiled the sweetest smile I'd ever seen. I cooled down a little and heard the priest ask, "Are you sure you want to name him Jesus? Why not name him Joseph after yourself or one of the patriarchs?"

Mary was still smiling at me. I couldn't say what I wanted to say, so as calmly as I could, I said, "His name is Jesus." To this he said nothing. He didn't need to. His look said, *So you're going to try to perpetuate this crazy story!* But he went on with his job. When he was finished, we left immediately and went straight home.

Our new home was on the edge of town, somewhat apart from other houses. When we got into the house and put Jesus down, I hugged Mary tightly and murmured, "Thanks for helping me. I almost blew it! Would have, if you hadn't looked at me the way you did."

"I was just as upset as you, but I remembered what you said, 'This is God's son. It's His job to announce him, promote him. Not ours,' " she murmured soothingly.

After a few moments I chimed in again, "Well, you better start saving up your courage and strength and some more smiles like that! In about a month we have to go to Jerusalem to make an offering there. Who knows what will happen then?"

11

The Recognition

Josiah came by that evening as he did almost every day, either going to or coming from his sheep. As he came in he stopped and listened for a moment, "Isn't Jesus here?" he asked.

"Of course," Mary told him, "why do you think he isn't?"

"He's not crying? Hmmm, that's strange! My little brother was circumcised last month and he cried for a week." He looked at Mary questioningly.

Mary just smiled back at him, but said nothing. She didn't want to brag on her baby. Then she said, "Well, Jesus did and does cry sometimes...a little, but..."

Josiah said, "I thought so!" He was quiet for a moment then added, "Yeah, since this is the child the angels told us about, why wouldn't he be special?"

It was so good to have one friend who trusted you and believed you! Most other people were polite, but Josiah was really a friend to us.

As the routines of life overtook us, the days turned into weeks, the weeks into a month. And before we knew it, it was time to go to Jerusalem.

We weren't looking forward to it. Actually, we were dreading it. Life had become tolerable in Bethlehem once again, like it was before Jesus was born. The people, while not overly friendly, were willing to speak to us. At least they didn't look on us as Samaritans or foreigners anymore. But what would happen in Jerusalem? As devout Jews, we were required to go to the Temple and present Jesus there. We also had to make the purification offering for Mary. Still we dreaded the trip, expecting the worst.

On the actual day of the journey, we got up very early. As we were getting ready, I prayed, "Lord, help me to be an encouragement to Mary today. You know we are both dreading this trip...dreading what might happen. Help me to lighten her load. You know how much I love her...help me to show it in a meaningful way. And Lord, bless your Son!"

We left the house just as the sun was coming up. It looked like it would be a beautiful day. For a little while, we were both lost in our thoughts. I suppose she, like me, was wondering what would happen in Jerusalem. *If I'm going to cheer her up, I'd better get started,* I thought.

"You know, I've been thinking...," I said.

Before I could say more, Mary laughed. "That's dangerous!" she said with a twinkle in her eye. "What were you thinking about?"

"Well, do you remember what we were doing last time we took a journey like this?"

"How could I forget? Traveling to Bethlehem...what a time that was! Our hopes were high; we were just married." Then Mary sighed. "It seems we've been so busy lately, we've hardly had time to remember God's blessings."

"That's what I was thinking. Do you remember comparing our 'angel' stories? I'm glad we were by ourselves and not in a group. People would have really thought we were strange if they'd heard us talking," I finished with a laugh.

Mary smiled thoughtfully and quietly replied, "I remember the love and trust in God we discovered in each other, and how He brought us together."

So we talked, remembering all the good things God had done in our lives. We didn't mention—or worry about—the difficult times because we could see God's hand in it all. It was good to hear Mary's voice lift, hear her humming a little tune, and see the worry lines in her face begin to disappear. I thanked God for helping me lift her spirits. Mine were lifted, too. With hearts, minds and souls now rejoicing, we continued on our journey, ready for the difficulties we expected.

When we reached Jerusalem, we set out to buy the sacrifice offering for Mary. We had considered getting a lamb from Josiah, but we didn't want to bother with it on the trip. Instead, we decided to buy one at the Temple in Jerusalem. What we didn't expect was the high price. The only thing we could afford was a couple of doves, and I was barely able to manage that. Well, at least Mary knew I was poor before we were married! It didn't seem to bother her, but it bothered me —especially when I noticed that no one else had such a lowly offering. "What next, Lord?" I muttered.

In the Temple, things went a bit better. At least no one knew us so there were none of those 'knowing' glances that we had come to expect in Bethlehem. However, when the priest saw our simple offering, he gave me a look that seemed to say, "I'll not get any money out of this one!" He was right, of course, but there was nothing I could do except look embarrassed.

After our offering was made—as we were leaving the sacrifice area—an old man came tottering up to us. He blocked our way, almost tripping me with his cane, his eyes fixed on the baby. Then, before I knew what was happening, he dropped his cane, grabbed Jesus from Mary's arms and began shouting. I stooped to pick up the cane with the unholy urge to beat him with it. But I couldn't—he had Jesus in his arms! As Mary held out her hand to calm me down, I heard what he was saying.

...I have seen your salvation you have prepared for all people. He is a light to reveal God to the nations, and he is the glory of your people Israel![12]

The old man was praising God!

I was dumbfounded. Someone actually recognized Jesus for who he was! By this time, a crowd had gathered around us. I expected them to pick up stones and begin throwing them. Instead, they looked curious and respectful. I suppose

---

[12]Luke 2:30-32

they knew who the man was and had a lot of respect for him. Later, I learned his name was Simeon and recalled seeing him at the temple on earlier visits. Mary also told me later that while I was picking up his walking stick, he said, "Sovereign Lord, now let your servant die in peace, as you promised me."[13]

At the time, though, Mary and I were bewildered. As the crowd looked on, we looked at each other and then at Simeon, who was looking intently at Jesus. I'm not sure if those around us actually heard what Simeon said, or just came because of the commotion. Maybe they wondered what I intended to do with his walking stick! Nevertheless, after a few moments of silence, Simeon took his eyes off Jesus, handed him back to Mary and the whole crowd sighed in relief. As I returned his walking stick to him, Simeon said to Mary,

> This child is destined to cause many in Israel to fall, but he will be a joy to many others. He has been sent as a sign from God, but many will oppose him. As a result, the deepest thoughts of many hearts will be revealed.[14]

He paused for a moment, looked down at the floor, then back

---

[13]Luke 2:29

[14]Luke 2:34-35a

at Mary. With tears in his eyes, he added,

"And a sword will pierce your very soul."[15]

I had put my arm around Mary while he was speaking and, at these words, I felt her body shudder. It took a moment for his message to sink in, but when it did, it felt like someone had slapped us in the face.

"Why?..." "Where...?" I began, but Simeon was gone. He had faded into the crowd, which was respectfully silent. A few of them looked at Jesus and made comments like, "What a beautiful baby!" or "How sweet!" It helped take some of the sting away.

Just as the group was beginning to disperse, a prophetess, Anna, approached. At first I figured she had come to add her 'sweet nothings' to the others. But, as I watched her look at Jesus, I could see worship and adoration in her face. Instead of fussing over him, she gave thanks to God and spoke about this special child. She told of how he would bring redemption to Jerusalem.

Everyone listened carefully. You could tell they had great respect for her. Though they seemed to believe Anna's words, they did not worship Jesus. That surprised me. Perhaps, deep inside, they just couldn't believe the old prophesies would be

---

[15]Luke 2:35b

fulfilled in this way. Perhaps, when they looked at Mary and me and saw how poor we were, they didn't want to believe it. Or maybe they thought the old prophetess was finally losing her mind. The one thing they failed to do was look—really look—at Jesus. In my heart I prayed, "Oh, God, help your people look to Jesus, not at all the people and things and situations around them. What will it take, Lord, to get them to see your Truth?"

After such a dramatic morning and having spent most of our money on those two little doves, I was emotionally—and financially—wiped out. So we began the journey back to Bethlehem without any lunch, our hearts filled with conflicting thoughts.

I suppose you could say we lacked faith at that point. Perhaps we did. We had God's son in our arms, yet for us to proclaim that meant getting even stranger looks, isolation from the community, and possibly even physical abuse. It's difficult to describe how we felt.

Literally everyone in the Jewish community knew of the prophecies regarding the Messiah. People prayed for Messiah to come, every girl dreamed of being the mother of the Messiah, but no one, it seemed, expected it to happen like it did. Perhaps no one had really expected it to happen at all. I remember questioning Mary's father about why God seemed so slow in fulfilling His prophecies. I prayed again, "Oh, God, help me to trust you for the impossible!"

That day's events only compounded our emotional stress. First, Simeon's recognition of Jesus had made our spirits soar. Then came his pronouncement of the pain that Mary would experience, which sobered us both. *Why didn't Simeon include me in that pain?* I wondered.

Though somewhat heartened by Anna's message, we were, by that time, emotionally drained. So rather than staying in Jerusalem and risking more ups and downs, we headed home. Home to Bethlehem. There, at least, we had weathered the storm of suspicion. At least there we could live in peace.

12

The Visit

Back in Bethlehem, we settled into a routine that kept us busy—too busy to worry about the future. The carpentry business picked up. Following the exodus, there was an excess of housing—most of it pretty run down. The bulk of my work came from those who wanted these places fixed up. Some of the folks in the sheep raising business occasionally needed more space for shearing and processing, so this also provided jobs from time to time. We lived comfortably, certainly better than my shack in Nazareth or the stable/cave here.

Like most babies, Jesus grew, and was soon toddling

around, getting into everything. He was very curious and would study something for hours until he figured it out. It was a completely new experience for me. As an only child I had, in my adult life, few opportunities to be around children—up to now. Even though my friend James in Nazareth had several daughters, I had seldom been with them. My long hours of work didn't leave much time for visiting with friends. Now, I was seeing the world a new way, through the eyes of a child.

I could hardly wait to get Jesus into the carpentry shop and teach him everything I knew. With his curiosity and patience, I knew Jesus would make a first class carpenter. Sometimes when Mary needed to go into the village, I'd take him into the shop and show him all the tools and talk about how fulfilling it was to make things from wood. He, in turn, loved to play with the shavings from the plane or in the sawdust. We would forget about the time and often Mary would return before we had time to clean up. She'd look at me with concern and say, "Joseph, are you trying to make a carpenter out of him? You know..."

Yes, I knew he wouldn't be a carpenter! But I could only teach him what I knew. And it was my responsibility as a father to teach him some trade. I also had a feeling that I might not have a long time with him, so I determined to give him a 'feel' for carpentry as early as possible.

The most important thing I wanted to teach Jesus was to be honest. Carpenters who did a poor job and charged a high price disgusted me. Or those who quoted one price and raised it because, they said, it took more time or the price of wood was going up or there was a shortage of something. Perhaps this was why I never became wealthy! Those carpenters gave our profession such a bad name, I guess I tried to compensate for them all. Instead of quoting a low price to get the job and later raising it, I would quote a slightly higher price and hope I could lower it. I suppose some would say I was a poor businessman. Perhaps. Regardless, I determined to be honest whether it hurt or not.

You would think that once my honesty became known, smart people would flock to my shop. But they didn't. If I heard it once, I heard it a thousand times, "But I talked to Malchus (or someone else) on the other side of town and he can do the same job for half that." I knew that Malchus couldn't, or wouldn't, but I would smile and say very politely, "Then by all means have Malchus do the job for you." Actually I had to be careful what I said. It would have been easy to speak badly of my fellow carpenters—and I admit I was sorely tempted! But before God, I just couldn't.

With a bit of pride, I must confess, that many times people told me, "You're a good man, Joseph. You're honest!"

Ah, that was nice to hear, even though it meant having matzo ball soup instead of *chicken* and matzo ball soup!

One evening about dusk, just as we were sitting down to give thanks for the soup (without the meat), there was a commotion outside. I heard shouts, the noise of a crowd, and then heard the clop, clop, clop of camels. I dislike being disturbed at mealtime, but since we seldom saw camels in Bethlehem — especially so close to our house — curiosity pulled me away from the dinner table.

About the time I got up, the sound of the camels stopped. For a moment I was afraid I'd missed them. But, when I opened the door to see what was happening, there was the crowd—it looked like the whole village of Bethlehem—and behind them I saw the heads and humps of camels! At that moment, the crowd parted and three men who looked like kings appeared.

I turned back into the house to call Mary—she wasn't interested in camels, so had not come to the door. "Mary, come quickly! They're coming here! Quickly!"

When I turned around, the kings arrived at the door. Each had a gift in his hands and the first one walked hand in hand with Jesus. *How did he get outside?* I was dumbfounded. They were strange looking people—I'd never seen anyone dressed the way they were. My first instinct was to block the door. But Jesus was with them—I couldn't refuse them entry. Reluctantly, I stepped aside to let them in. As I did, Mary gasped and clapped her hand over her mouth, her eyes wide open. She was as awestruck as I was.

Finally, I found my tongue and asked, "Were you looking for someone in particular?" Yeah, I know it's a stupid question, but remember I'm just a carpenter. I'd never even seen a king before, much less had one in my house! I didn't know who they were or where they came from or even if they were really kings.

As I stood there wondering, one of them spoke: "We have come from the East to worship the King of the Jews who was born here."

"We've been on the road for many days since his star appeared," said another.

"We stopped in Jerusalem and learned from King Herod that according to the scriptures, the king was to be born here," the third added.

Suddenly, my tongue was released and I began praising God for this recognition of His son! Then I said to them, "This is our son Jesus. Actually, he's God's son. The night he was born, shepherds came to visit us and said that an angel had announced his birth to them and that a choir of angels sang praises to God. When the shepherds saw the baby, they worshiped him. But the town's people..."

I was about to tell how the people of Bethlehem had rejected him, but my voice trailed off as the kings fell to their knees in front of Jesus. After a while, they stood up. One by one, with heads bowed, they handed their gifts to Jesus, who by then had climbed into Mary's arms.

As each gift was opened, we gasped in awe. I doubt that anyone in Bethlehem had ever seen such riches as these. Each box was like a small treasure chest and when the box was opened, the gift inside lay there for all to see. There was gold—I had never imagined there was that much gold in the world! Frankincense, a costly perfume! And Myrrh! The crowd, watching through the door and windows, gasped as each beautifully decorated gift was revealed.

The stately kings backed away and again knelt before Jesus and worshiped. I've always wondered what they actually thought. Perhaps they were as surprised as we were. We had never seen such riches—they had probably never seen such poverty. But they were kingly in their response. They accepted Jesus as the person they expected. What was even more surprising—even for Mary and me—and we knew who Jesus was—was how Jesus earnestly accepted the worship. When I look back on that scene, I can only laugh. Here was royalty bowing in worship to a child not quite two years old. The three men dressed in sumptuous robes. Jesus, on the other hand, barefoot and dressed in a knit shirt that was so small on him it was almost indecent. It was unbelievable!

About that time, I began to wonder what we should do. We had no room to offer them hospitality. We certainly didn't have enough soup to share. I looked at Mary with a questioning look, but realized that she was still in shock. *What to do? What do you offer a king?* In my desperation, I looked to heaven for a moment and silently prayed, "God, help me!"

At that very instant, Jesus went to each king, took his hand and seemed to indicate that he should rise. When they were all standing, Jesus moved to the door and they walked out. It was as simple as that.

As they were leaving, I saw that not only were there camels, but there were donkeys, pack horses and many servants—a whole caravan. The crowd seemed confused for a moment, wondering whether to stay at the house or follow the kings. The kings won. I suppose the townspeople figured that since we lived in Bethlehem, they could come and see us or the gifts anytime.

112

13

The Second Journey

We had lived in Bethlehem about two years before the kings visited. I had built a regular clientele which gave us enough to live on. More and more Bethlehem felt like home. Although we had few close friends, we seemed to be accepted in the community—or at least tolerated. I felt it was time to have other children. Mary wasn't so sure until one evening, at the supper table I shared some good news.

"Mary, I believe the innkeeper is going ahead with his plans to enlarge the inn. If he does, he said he'll give me the job."

"It's about time!" she retorted. "He's been talking about doing that ever since we came. Wasn't that one of the reasons he suggested that we stay in the stable, so he'd have free labor?"

"Hmm, perhaps so...he's a pretty cautious person. Kinda like we've been about having other children," I added.

She looked at me with a twinkle in her eyes, but didn't say anything. I knew I'd finally won that battle.

The next day was the day the kings came. I still call them kings for lack of a better word, but I never really knew who they were. I supposed they came to reaffirm in our minds that Jesus was a very special person. Of course, later, I was to learn more.

After the visit of the kings, the whole town was in an uproar. People talked about nothing else. They didn't know how to treat me. Clearly, I was now the richest man in the village—a difficult fact for the townspeople to accept. One day I was one of the poorest and looked down on by all...the next day I was the richest. Before, they despised me for my poverty, now they seemed to despise me for the wealth.

The day after the kings' visit, I went to work as usual. As people passed by the place of my current job, snippets of their conversations reached my ears..."Why him and not me?" "Who does he think he is?" "Guess he's too good for us now!"

It was a bad day, hard to keep my mind on my work and hard to ignore the remarks. I was also worrying about the kings' gifts. I finally stopped working and went home.

"What's wrong, Joseph? Are you sick?" Mary had seen me walking, or perhaps better, trudging home with my tools and had come out to meet me.

"No, not sick, just...oh, I don't know. I suppose...just bothered."

"What about?"

"I really don't know...perhaps it's the unkindness and curiosity of the people here, perhaps it's the gifts we received...What are we going to do with them?...Oh, I don't know...it's everything!" In frustration, I dropped my tool bag on the ground.

Mary looked at me, puzzled at my confusion, but said nothing.

"How soon can we eat? I think I'll get to bed early tonight."

"We can eat most anytime, Joseph," she replied gently. "I'll go prepare it now."

As Mary went in to get supper ready, I reached down to pick up my tool bag and realized Jesus had taken out all the tools and was looking at them. I got down on the ground with him.

Picking up one I said, "This is a block plane."

"Bok pain."

"Yes, this is a bLock pLane and it works like this..." Picking up a small tree limb, I showed in a few strokes how to make it smooth and square instead of round.

"Now this is a small axe or hatchet," I said as I used it to little twig to make a point on one end and then I drove it into the ground. Jesus picked up some of the chips and tried to stick them into the ground.

"Can you say, 'Axe'?"

"Aaks..." he repeated, as he chopped with his hand.

"And this is a hammer. You take a nail and pound these two pieces of wood together, like this. Can you say 'hammer'?"

"Amme."

When Mary called us in to supper, Jesus was looking at the little cross we had just made. He pulled it out of the ground and lifted it up to me with a questioning look.

"Yes, you can take it in." I scooped him up with the tools and went around to the back of the cottage to wash up.

We did get to bed early that evening, but the meal and the playtime with Jesus had revived me. I couldn't get to sleep. After tossing and turning for a while, I was suddenly aware of someone else in the room. I glanced over at Mary. She was sleeping peacefully. *Was I dreaming?* I wondered.

Rubbing my eyes, I looked across the room. It was the angel who had visited me before. I tried to speak, ask him who he was, but nothing came out; I could only stare and wonder.

Giving no greeting or salutation, the angel spoke as if continuing his previous message to me. He gave a simple message and warning:

Get up! Flee to Egypt with the child and his mother. Stay there until I tell you to return, because Herod is going to search for the child to kill him.[16]

He vanished and I woke up. Completely!

Quickly, I thought through what to take and how to travel. Then I touched Mary, "Mary, wake up! I just heard from the angel again."

Stirring from a deep sleep, she murmured, "Whaaat?"

"I just heard from the angel again. Jesus is in danger." I whispered. "We have to leave here tonight...right now!"

She looked at me questioningly, but the urgency in my voice finally sank in. "Okay, I'll get Jesus...and our things together..."

"Thanks, Mary. I'll get Jehu ready and the gifts the kings brought." Our hearts racing, we didn't light any lamps, but worked quickly, quietly, and urgently in the moonlight that

---

[16]Matthew 2:13

shone dimly thru the windows.

Fifteen minutes later, leading Jehu, we left Bethlehem with everything we owned. Well, almost everything. We left a few things, the furniture and some odds and ends, but so what? I was a carpenter and could make more.

The stars were shining brightly and the moon was up about one quarter. Not a bad night for a journey. It would be at least four, maybe five hours before the sun came up and by that time we should be almost at Hebron.

As we walked, an unpleasant thought struck me. I hadn't been paid for my last few jobs! How were we going to make a trip to Egypt? Traveling in Israel was one thing. You could expect to find hospitable people along the way to help out...but in Egypt? *If I'd been paid, I'd have enough money to at least get us into Egypt. Where in Egypt are we going, anyway?* These and other thoughts came rushing into my mind. I was just about to get warm under my tunic when a new thought hit me. *Whoa, Joseph! What about the gifts from the kings!* Then I smiled and began to whistle.

"What are you so happy about?" Mary asked. I told her what I'd been thinking earlier and she said, "So, what's so happy about that?'

"Well, suddenly I realized another reason the kings came." After I explained, Mary smiled. Then Jehu 'hee-hawed' like he was laughing, too, and we all joined in.

About an hour later, Mary spoke up, "Joseph, I'm not too sure about going to Egypt. Actually, I'm a little afraid."

I realized that the angel had only spoken to me this time, so I put my arm around her and answered gently, "My dear Mary, don't be afraid. No doubt we will face some hardships, but I'm convinced that our great God is leading us—that He will provide for us all along the way."

She seemed to accept that and we continued our journey in silence. Every now and then, though, Jehu would nudge one of us from behind like he was pushing us along and we'd both start laughing again.

As my thoughts reflected on the events of the past weeks, I began to wonder what Josiah would think when he discovered us gone? I knew he would miss us but, I thought, he'd probably be the only one who would. Little did I realize just how much we would be missed.

120

14

The Foreign Country

The angel's message was simple: "Go to Egypt." He didn't say where in particular to go or how to live there, nor did he say how long we were to stay.

I had never been to Egypt and wasn't looking forward to going there. After all, any Jew who knew their nation's history knew about the dark years of slavery in Egypt. Still, we traveled as fast as we could. Our son—God's Son—was in danger. I remembered something that Mary's father had said to me: "I'm afraid your faith will be tested many times in the days to come." How true that was now!

Had we had time to plan, we might have taken a different route. But not wanting to get lost in the wilderness we chose to take well-traveled routes. From the urgency in the angel's message, I was afraid we might see soldiers on the road, but we didn't. I could only suppose that Herod heard about the "King of the Jews," as the kings referred to Jesus, from our royal visitors. But when did they tell him? I was sure that they set off in the opposite direction from Jerusalem when they left. As I wondered, we continued our journey southward towards Egypt.

We chose carefully where to stop each evening. Assuming we were being pursued, we avoided good sized cities, stopping instead in little villages where we could purchase some food and find a place to sleep. Since we looked so poor, no one welcomed us until I showed them a gold coin. Over and over we thanked God for providing for our needs!

After we'd been on the road for about two weeks and were well into Egypt, we came to a small town. The people were kind and friendly. Sure, they stared at us since we weren't Egyptians, but the looks we received were different—better than in Bethlehem. We decided to stay for a while.

Jesus and Mary became the center of attention wherever we went. Everyone had something to say about Jesus—what a good little boy he was. And they were more inquisitive than the people had ever been in Bethlehem. Maybe it was because we were foreigners.

After we were settled, I got out my tools and tried to find work. I really didn't need to work since we had the gifts the kings gave us, but I thought it would look odd if I didn't. It wouldn't fit with our look of poverty. Anyhow, idleness didn't suit me. We didn't stay long enough in one place to set up a real business, but there were a few good jobs. I always found opportunities to do small repairs for someone in exchange for something to eat.

Altogether, we lived in four towns during our sojourn in Egypt. We would stay in one place for several months until I began to feel uncomfortable. *What if someone is following us? What if they are searching in Egypt for us?* Except for these occasional nervous spells and our moves, it was a relaxed time in our lives. We were never hassled by any of our unbelieving brothers which was a blessing.

Jesus spent lots of time with me and the tools. I told him all I knew about carpentry. I'm sure he didn't understand everything, but he showed keen interest and his company made the days go faster.

Another thing we enjoyed was admiring the treasure boxes the kings had given us. The craftsmanship was exquisite. Each joint was perfectly fitted and joined. The inlaid wood of different colors and jewels were beautiful to behold. It was not my kind of craft, but I admired it greatly. We kept one of the boxes on the shelf for people to admire— never all of them, only one at a time. People would notice it and ask questions. Thankfully, due to language differences our communication was limited, so I never really had to say much. Finally, someone would show a special interest and, after coming back several times, would purchase the little treasure chest. When we moved to a different village, we'd put another one out and the process would begin all over again.

We took special care to keep the gold and the other gifts hidden. I didn't want to tempt anyone. Gradually, as we moved from place to place, we sold off all the gifts to meet our needs.

My desire to grow a family was fulfilled in Egypt. One of our happiest days there was the day little James was born! This time an Egyptian mid-wife helped Mary, so I was able to enjoy the people who came to see what a Jewish baby looked like. The Egyptian women babbled advice to Mary on how to care for James, like she had never had a baby before. Mary was kind and listened graciously to their suggestions. Using sign language, she tried to show some of her visitors how Jewish mothers did things, but they just laughed like they'd never heard anything so funny.

This time there was no question about our baby boy's name. I'd made a promise to my best friend.

"Thank you, LORD," I prayed, "for this son, James, you have given me. Now I feel your blessing on me. I have trusted you for many years, but now I feel it since you have blessed me with my own son. May your mighty name be praised."

When James was eight days old, as there was no priest around, I had to do the circumcising. After that, when the Egyptian 'helpers' would change the baby's clothes or bathe him, there would be a gasp and concerned questions. We could never make them understand the reason or significance for circumcision. We didn't know enough of their language and they didn't know enough of ours. Finally, it came to the point where we would simply lift our shoulders and shrug and they'd shake their heads incredulously.

Three-year-old Jesus was a big help to Mary. He was fascinated with little James and spent hours entertaining him. Actually, now I had to coax Jesus to help in the carpentry work. When I'd call him, he'd say, "Can I bring James with me?"

"No, he's a little too young," I'd say.

After a few minutes, Jesus would poke his head out the door and explain that he had to say goodbye to James before he could come. But once he came, he'd turn his full attention to me and the 'work' we did together.

While we worked, I told Jesus stories from the Scriptures. This was our substitute for the lack of a synagogue to attend. I started it as Scriptural training for Jesus, but as I related events in the lives of Abraham, Moses, Joshua, and the others, I learned more about God myself. Jesus especially enjoyed the stories about Joseph in Egypt. Occasionally, he would convince Mary and me to act out some part of the story while he played the part of Joseph. Mary was good at this, but I was a terrible actor. Even if I knew the story well, I always messed up my lines. I could never put the motion and the words together in a convincing way. So usually, before we could finish a story, we'd all be laughing at my expense. But that was okay. We had great fun as we 'lived' the stories of the Scriptures together.

One day many months later, while Jesus was out playing with some village children and James was asleep, Mary came out to my work place. She stood there for a while watching me work. At first she just watched, making me nervous. After a bit she said, "I just love to watch you work with wood. You move so smoothly. It's like you love the wood."

That warmed my heart! After that, I was never again

concerned about my shortcomings. It was true, I did love the wood.

Then she finally mentioned what was worrying her, "Joseph, when do you think we can finish OUR wilderness wanderings?" she whispered plaintively. The day before I had told Jesus about the children of Israel who had wandered in the wilderness for forty years. When I looked up from my work, I saw tears in Mary's eyes. Before I could think of what to say, she went on.

"I'm so tired of this desert land, the sand, the wind, the heat...," she paused for a moment, then added, "Bethlehem sounds so wonderful right now!"

The plough handle I was working on could wait. I laid it down, went to Mary and wrapped my arms around her. She was carrying child number three now—I was hoping for another boy so I could finally have a namesake.

After a moment, she murmured into my shoulder, "I'm so tired of moving around from place to place. Couldn't we just settle down somewhere?"

"Well, I..." I began, but she interrupted.

"I wish I had somebody to talk to. The women here are nice, but it's so hard to carry on a conversation."

Then she burst out crying and through her tears cried, "I want to see my family!"

"Oh, Mary..." was all I could say at the moment. I realized then how much more difficult living in Egypt was for her than for me. I had no family but her and the boys. As I thought about her loneliness, tears came to my eyes. Not only did they wash the sawdust out of them, but I began to see the situation from her point of view.

As I started to respond, she interrupted me again. "Thanks for understanding, Joseph. I know we can't leave here till God gives us direction. I'll be okay. Besides," she patted her tummy, "with little Joseph here we can't travel too far, can we?" She must have read my mind. She looked at me with a twinkle in her eyes and a smile on her face. Then we kissed and she went back into the house. I determined right then that we'd stay put, right where we were, until we knew it was safe to go back home.

A few months later, my namesake was born. Again, there was great excitement over the birth of a baby and once again we went through the questions and strange looks after little Joseph was circumcised. This time we knew what to expect, told them it was our custom, and left it at that.

Forty days after Joseph's birth—about the time I had to apologize to the Lord for not being able to offer the sacrifices for Mary's cleansing—an angel appeared once again and said to me,

Get up! Take the child and his mother back to the land of Israel, because those who were trying to kill the child are dead.[17]

Though it was the middle of the night, I praised God fervently, but quietly, for his blessings, for keeping us safe in a strange land, for the two 'Egyptian' sons he had given us. There were so many things to be thankful for, I didn't ask for anything. Then, after an hour, I went back to sleep with a rejoicing heart.

---

[17]Matthew 2:20

130

15

The Return

Early the next morning I got up before anyone else and began preparing for our trip. I wondered what it would be like to be back in Bethlehem. We'd have our own little house—I hoped we could get our house back! We'd only been gone a few years. Whoever was in it would just have to move! The more I thought about going home, the more excited I became. I even began singing out loud—I couldn't help myself! I hadn't gotten through the first verse before Mary came bounding out of the house.

"Joseph, Joseph! Please! Your singing is enough to raise

the..." She stopped short, looking at the donkeys which were harnessed and the big smile on my face. "What's going on? Where are you going? Why..." she began.

I held up my hand to stop the continuous flow of questions, looked into her eyes and said, "How would you like to go back to Bethlehem?"

"Bethlehem!" she said wistfully, "I was just asking the Lord this morning if perhaps we could go home soon...Oh, Joseph...Bethlehem! How soon can we leave?"

"As soon as we're ready!"

"Oh," she cried, "I'll get the boys up and get things packed!"

With that she raced back to the house and was almost inside before I could say, "What about breakfast?"

She spun around. "If I didn't know you better, I'd think that all you think about is your stomach!" she exclaimed, half glaring at me. But then she winked and came running back, reached up, put her arms around my neck, and whispered in my ear, "I love you, Joseph."

I held her for a moment, then felt her stiffen. Suddenly she looked up at me, questions and fear on her face. I smiled tenderly and said, "An angel visited me last night and..."

Before I could say any more, she broke from my arms and said with excitement in her voice, "We'll talk about the angel later—there'll be plenty of time on the road. Let's get going!" When she got to the door she paused, turned around and said mischievously, "What does the hungry man want for breakfast?"

"Anything you fix will be heavenly!" I exclaimed, at which she let out a "Psshaaw" and winked at me again. Jehu didn't 'hee-haw,' but he was shaking his head up and down like he knew what was going on—or maybe I'd drawn the cinch too tight.

It wasn't long before we were on the road. We had packed up and moved so many times we knew precisely what to do. Jesus was a big help, but the two little boys needed a lot of attention.

Once we were on the road Mary asked about the angel's visit. Jesus was getting old enough to understand more about some of the events that had shaped our lives. He was especially interested in knowing why we could now return to our home, so we shared it all with him. As we rehearsed the story once again, adding the part about the death of King Herod, he was clearly upset by the killing of infant boys in Bethlehem. His response this time really shook me. I expected a response like, 'Bad, ole wicked King!' Instead, Jesus asked the question Mary and I had hoped he would never ask: "Papa, did King Herod want to kill me?"

How should I answer that question? What could I say to a five-year-old child? How much could he really understand? I didn't know the answers, but was determined to be truthful. Just as I opened my mouth to respond to his question, Mary put her hand on my arm. Her look said, "Do you have to tell him?" She wanted to protect him, but I knew in my heart he would find out some day. Then, Jesus tugged at my tunic. He looked up at me, his searching eyes wondering if I was going to answer his question. So I answered truthfully, "Yes, Jesus, I believe he was."

He looked like someone had hit him in the stomach as he let out an "Oh...!" He stumbled and almost fell, but I put my hand on his shoulder to steady him. His body felt hot and tense. I looked over at Mary. She was holding little Joseph and tears flooded her eyes. Both of us wanted to say something to lift his spirits, but neither of us knew what to say. Slowly, Jesus began to relax and I moved my hand to his head and combed my fingers through his hair. After a few more minutes he said questioningly, "Papa...?"

"Yes, my son?"

"Do you think God still loved King Herod even after he had all those babies killed?"

I was dumbfounded! How should I answer that? "Well...I

know that one of the things God hates is 'hands that shed innocent blood'..."

Jesus interrupted, "But that's just his hands. I'm sure God still loved him!" And with that he started skipping merrily ahead of us like everything in the world was okay. I looked over at Mary. Her mouth hung open in amazement.

I laughed to myself and said to her, "Trying to catch bugs for supper?" Her head jerked around to me, her mouth closed, and her eyes, wide with astonishment, narrowed for a second to a piercing glare. I just smiled at her. Then we both started laughing, James started clapping his hands and even Jehu let out a 'hee-haw'. Little Joseph? He slept through it all.

Well, we might as well be happy, I thought. We were certainly no longer rich. The frankincense, the myrrh, and the three little chests the gifts came in were all gone—sold to pay for our life in Egypt. Most of the gold had also been spent. Work had been even more difficult to get than in Israel, mostly because we didn't stay long enough in one place to build up a business.

That whole day we talked about home. We were overjoyed to be returning to Bethlehem. Jesus couldn't wait to meet Josiah since we had told him all about his friendship. Mary talked about our family being in our own little house again. And I began planning how to add another room to the house. All these things filled our minds and our hearts as we trod toward home.

The next day my mind turned to other things. Perhaps reality set in. For example, I wondered how the people of Bethlehem would respond to us. Would they welcome us as the rich people who left them? Or, would they still despise us—not for our poverty...or our riches—but because we ran out on them and escaped the slaughter of all the baby boys? Perhaps they would think our riches could have been their salvation. We didn't talk as much that day.

On the third day, our excitement grew once again. I figured we would be in Israel before nightfall—our first night in our homeland in almost three years.

One of the most difficult parts of living in Egypt was not knowing what was happening back in Israel. Sure, there were lots of Jews in Egypt at that time, working in the fields or doing other jobs to make money. But we avoided them as much as possible, not knowing who they might be connected with. We heard about the slaughter of the babies in Bethlehem, but little else. So, naturally, when we crossed the border into Israel—in the first town we came to—we eagerly asked for the latest news.

16

The Plans Change

Yes, King Herod had died. Just four days ago! We had been on the road for three days, so the angel had delivered the message right on time. The unfortunate news was that Archelaus was reigning in Judea in place of Herod, his father. The people I talked to were not sure if this was better or worse, but they feared the worst. I was afraid, as well.

We stayed in a small inn that night. This time there was room in the inn, Mary was not expecting—or at least not that I was aware of!—we were not in a hurry, and there seemed to be peace around us. Mary had been settling in and getting the children ready for bed while I was out talking and getting the latest news. She sensed my uneasiness as soon as I returned.

"What's wrong, Joseph?"

"Oh, nothing really, I guess I'm just tired."

"You're only tired because something is troubling you. I know you! What's happened?"

I never tried to hide anything from Mary, but I wasn't anxious to add to her burdens. I realized, though, that I would have to share it eventually. "Okay, as soon as the boys get to sleep, we'll talk."

As she bustled about getting James and Jesus bedded down on the mats, I went to check on the donkeys. As I left Jesus gave me a puzzled glance, but said nothing.

The donkeys were fine, of course, I just wanted to think and pray about how to break the news to Mary. Was I being overly sensitive and not trusting God? I talked this all over with God while I puttered around with the donkeys.

Yes, we had two of them now. And were they misnamed! We named the donkey we bought in Egypt Eli. Jehu was now the wise old donkey, while Eli was the young and rambunctious one! I gave them a pat and walked back to the inn.

When I returned to our room, the boys were settled on

their mats and Mary was across the room sewing. I sat down, looked at her and smiled at the disinterested look she tried to project. I knew she was curious, but was trying to be patient.

"Are the boys asleep?"

"I think so, they've been quiet for several minutes now..." and she might have added, "while I've been waiting on you," but she didn't.

So I told her about Archelaus. After all the stalling, there really wasn't much to tell. We sat in silence for several minutes, both lost in thought.

Did God want us to walk into the fiery furnace? Was He going to show his majesty and protect us and his son by some miraculous means? We were not sure. Finally we prayed together, "Abba Father, we are afraid. Maybe we are not trusting you like we should, but we are afraid for ourselves and your son. Nevertheless, if you want us to go to Bethlehem we'll go. Just give us the assurance that you'll be with us."

When we finished praying, I sensed Jesus beside me. I hadn't heard him get up, but there he was, concern written all over his face. I smiled confidently at him. When he put his hand on mine, I picked him up, put him on my lap, and hugged him close to my heart. Neither of us said anything. We didn't need to. After a few minutes of silence, I said, "Okay, young man, I think it's past your bed time. Go give your mother a kiss and get back to bed."

"Okay, Papa!" He jumped down, gave Mary a big hug and kiss, looked her in the eyes and said, "I love you, Mama," turned to me said, "I love you, Papa," then he ran and jumped onto his bed.

Mary and I looked at each other. Then she got up, came over, and sat on my lap. We hugged each other tightly. Over the top of Mary's head I saw Jesus lift his head and look up at us. Then he smiled, laid back down, and went to sleep. I have to admit that I still had some doubts and fears about going to Bethlehem, but much more powerful than that was the assurance that God would take care of us.

When I woke up the next morning, I realized the angel had visited me again. He had warned me about going to Bethlehem, but he didn't give any specific instructions as to where to go. As I lay there in bed, I puzzled over the difference in this message. Always before there had been specific instructions—no, the last time in Egypt, the angel didn't tell me to return to Bethlehem. He had only said, "...take the child and his mother to the land of Israel." I had only assumed that we should go to Bethlehem! When I realized this, I sat up in bed and shouted, "Hallelujah!"

Mary, awakened out of sleep, said, "Joseph! What in the world...!"

Two other heads popped up and baby Joseph started crying.

Mary chortled, "Now look what you've done!"

I looked at her and said loudly over Joseph's crying, "How would you like to go home to Nazareth?"

Her eyes lit up, "Really? Nazareth?" I nodded and she shouted, "Hallelujah!" Joseph wailed louder. Jesus picked up James and joined us in our bed just as a man in the next room shouted, "Quiet down in there!" I put my finger to my lips and said, "Shhhhh." Mary did the same to me. Then Jesus did it to both of us. We started laughing. We laughed even louder when James tried to copy us, but couldn't get just one finger up to his lips and couldn't make the sound. All the while Joseph kept crying.

Mary looked at me and said, "One of us is going to have to get Joseph."

"Don't look at me," I said, "I've already got two boys on me."

"Well, he's your namesake!" But she smiled when she said it. She couldn't keep a straight face when she was joking. So she jumped up, got Joseph and brought him back to our bed. While Mary nursed Joseph, I told them all about the revelation and how we could go home—really home—to Nazareth.

When Jesus' questions began, I realized that we hadn't talked much about Nazareth. There was so much to tell! But now, we needed to get on the road, so I promised we'd talk as we traveled. I knew that time would pass quickly on our journey as we talked about home.

While I was getting some water skins and bread for the trip, I met another family who was going to Jerusalem and we agreed to caravan that far together. They would lead, we would follow, and at night we'd stay together. This would save a few of our last gold pieces and I figured that Jesus would enjoy being with other children his age.

So the trek to Nazareth began. Knowing that Jesus was anxious to learn more about Nazareth, as soon as we were on the road Mary asked him, "Guess what I'm looking forward to most about going back to Nazareth?"

Jesus answered immediately, "The house that you and Papa lived in when you were first married!" I had already told him about the house and the carpentry shop, but I knew that wasn't Mary's top item.

"No, guess again."

"I don't know." Jesus pulled my sleeve and looked at me like he was asking, "Do you know?" I nodded. So he whispered, "Tell me."

"Your grandmother and grandfather," I whispered in his ear.

When he repeated excitedly, "Your grandmother and grandfather!" Mary and I laughed. He had never met his grandparents. The only chance he might have had to see them was in Jerusalem at the Passover when he was one year old, but we had decided not to go. We weren't ready to meet our friends from Nazareth at that time. It was a little too soon.

Mary corrected him, "They are *your* grandmother and grandfather, but they are my mother and father, just like your papa and I are father and mother to you."

Jesus shook his head like he was trying to understand, then said, "Do other kids have grandfathers and grandmothers?"

"Oh, yes, all kids have them." Mary went into great detail describing her parents to Jesus. By the time we stopped at midday for a piece of bread and some water, Jesus was talking about his grandparents like he'd lived with them all his life.

When we found a little shade for our lunch break, Jesus ran over to meet the other kids and started out by saying, "I'm going to visit my grandparents. They..." I couldn't hear the rest because Hosea, the head of the family we were traveling with, came over to talk.

After lunch, Jesus asked to travel with the other family for a while, so Mary and I had some time to talk. Looking pensively at the ground she said, "Joseph, I've been thinking about us going to Jerusalem."

I interrupted her this time, "I've been thinking about that, too. We could stop there and make the sacrifice for you that the law requires, even if it is late. And I think Jesus would love to see the Temple."

"Yes, you're right, we could do that. But I was wondering if we could go and visit Elizabeth and Zachariah. Then you could meet Zachariah, and Jesus and John could meet each other. They are cousins, you know."

"That's a great idea. We'll do it! While we're at the Temple I can find out if Zachariah is on duty."

It seemed a good plan. We were excited.

17

The Side Trip

Jerusalem! Back on familiar territory, we easily found a good, but affordable place to spend the night. The next morning we made arrangements for our hostess to keep James and Joseph for a few hours while we went to the Temple. Our trek there brought back mixed memories of the first time Mary had come, except this time we had two lambs to offer. Thankfully, we had no problems as before.

Jesus was unusually quiet, studying everything. At first, he cautiously watched people, almost as if he expected someone to grab him. When we came to the Temple he was so impressed with its grandeur, he began running into people, his head thrown back and his eyes scanning the great building. Inside, Jesus was especially intrigued with the sacrifice offering and the words of the priest, although he seemed disturbed by the priest's lack of enthusiasm. Indeed, the priest didn't put much heart into the sacrifice but, I thought to myself, *at least he wasn't unpleasant.*

After we had completed our sacrifices, we learned that Zachariah was not on duty. So we returned to the inn, collected our things, said goodby to our hostess, and headed to Zachariah's home in the hill country. Now it was Mary's turn to lead the way—she had been here before. I took charge of the babies and the donkeys, while Jesus walked ahead with his mother. I knew she was telling him all about her last visit. From time to time one of them would look back and nod and smile.

Lost in thought of how to enlarge our little house in Nazareth, I was surprised when Mary called out, "We're here!" I looked up. The house we'd stopped at looked like a palace to me! I felt immediately uncomfortable. As Mary went in the gate and called for Elizabeth and Zachariah, I waited outside with the animals...like I was a servant.

Suddenly a high pitched, wailing voice pierced the air, "Maaarrrryy!" and a woman came running out of the house.

As she looked our way, the lowering sun glinted off her eyes and I sensed something was wrong. She hugged Mary and then noticed me at the gate. Turning, she called into the house, "Joash, come take care of Joseph's donkeys!" Then she invited me in. As I collected James and baby Joseph, I saw a sight that made my heart leap for joy. I had just heard Elizabeth say, "Is this Jesus?" Mary must have nodded because there was Elizabeth, kneeling down in front of Jesus. Tears flowed freely down her face.

Jesus said brightly, "Hi, Aunt Elizabeth. Mother told me all about you." He took her hand to help her up, but before she could get up Zachariah came out. When he saw what was happening, he too, dropped to his knees and said reverently, "Jesus, my Lord and my God!"

"Hi, Uncle Zachariah! Mother told me you couldn't talk, but you can!" he said, looking at Mary with a puzzled look.

While Elizabeth and Zachariah were getting up, Zachariah said, "Yes, that's true, I wasn't able to talk for several months. Do you want me to tell you about it?"

"Oh, yes!" he said excitedly, then added, "Where is cousin John?"

"Outside for sure! Where exactly, there is no telling. But he'll be here for supper. He wouldn't miss that!"

As I had just reached the porch with James and Joseph,

Mary introduced us, then added excitedly, "We were on our way home to Nazareth, but thought it would be good if John and Jesus could meet. And I so wanted Joseph to meet you."

Elizabeth took baby Joseph and responded, "We're glad you did, but let's go inside and get something for your feet." She spoke animatedly, but I noticed furtive glances between her and Zachariah.

It was blessedly cool inside. After we sat down, a maid came and washed our feet and gave us cloths to wash our face and hands. Oh, it was so good to be back in Israel where civilized customs were practiced! This was a first for Jesus and he looked at me, his eyes full of questions. I nodded to him and mouthed the words, "It's okay."

When the maid finished washing his feet, he asked her, "What's your name?"

She seemed astonished that he would ask, but responded, "Miriam."

"Thank you, Miriam!"

When he said that, she looked up at him for the first time and smiled. Suddenly, I was shocked as I realized I had taken the foot washing for granted. Slightly embarrassed, I mumbled, "Yes, uh, thank you, Miriam."

She gave us all a little bow and with a broad grin said, "You're welcome!" Then she gathered up her things and left us. Maybe I just imagined it, but it seemed she left us with a lighter step, a little happier than she was before, thanks to Jesus!

At the evening meal Zachariah presided over the reading of the Scriptures, praying for the peace of Israel and the breaking of the bread. I was amazed to see how sincerely and passionately Zachariah led this simple custom. My mind drifted back to earlier in the day and the priest at the Temple who had offered the sacrifices in such a perfunctory way. How different it would have been had Zachariah been there!

Jesus and John sat across the table from each other. Neither said much during the meal. They were very different. Jesus was kind and thoughtful and quiet. John was not unkind or unthoughtful, but he was definitely unquiet! I could imagine him growing up to be a popular, outgoing person that everyone liked.

"...Joseph?" I heard someone say. I looked up and realized that everyone was looking at me. Zachariah continued, "Joseph, Mary was telling us about your trip into Egypt." I looked at Mary and her eyes were shooting daggers at me for daydreaming, but before I could respond, John spoke up.

"He must have been dreaming about the leeks and garlics in Egypt!" And everyone laughed. Even me, after a little bit.

And so we talked about Egypt until the meal was finished and it was time to put the children to bed.

I excused myself to go check on the donkeys. Elizabeth started to speak, but she was interrupted by Zachariah saying, "I'll go with you."

I knew that was unusual and glanced at Mary who seemed to notice it as well, but she and Elizabeth went on talking. Zachariah followed me out—actually, I followed him out since I didn't know the way. As soon as we were outside, he turned around and said, "Joseph, the donkeys are all taken care of. Joash is really good with the animals. But I wanted a chance to tell you some bad news. Mary's parents are not living. They ..."

I almost fainted. My knees started to fold, and probably would have, had not Zachariah put his arms around me. "Easy, brother!" He said, as he held me up.

"I'm sorry. I..." my voice trailed off.

"It's okay. I know it's a shock to you, but if you take the news this hard, I hate to imagine how Mary will respond."

"Yes, I agree. Let's get back inside quickly." I wanted to be there when Mary heard the news. But I didn't quite make it.

Later, Mary told me that as soon as I left the room she had begun telling Elizabeth how excited she was to be heading home to see her parents after all the difficulties and the troubles in Egypt. Suddenly, she noticed that Elizabeth avoided looking at her. Finally, she asked Elizabeth if she had heard from her mom and dad recently. Elizabeth had no option but to tell her. Fortunately, Mary was still sitting at the table, when she heard the bad news.

She was sitting there, stunned, when Zachariah and I walked in. I ran to Mary, put my arms around her, held her and prayed. After a few more moments of silence, I said, "I think I'll take Mary to our room now. It's been a long day."

"Joseph," Elizabeth began, "I'm so sorry. I..."

"It's okay, Elizabeth." I led Mary to the room that had been prepared for us and we laid down, knowing that neither of us would sleep much that night.

18

The Sunshine

The next morning, I got up early and went to check on the boys. Baby Joseph was beginning to wake up and since I wanted the boys to sleep as long as possible, I scooped him up, cleaned him, dressed him in dry clothes, and took him to Mary. I hated to disturb her, but she was his only source of nourishment. I had no choice. When I laid Joseph beside her, she jerked awake. She grabbed Joseph, almost savagely, and hugged him so hard it scared me. Then she relaxed, cradled the baby so he could nurse and looked at me with tears in her eyes. I was afraid feeding Joseph might be too much for her, but instead, she smiled and said, "Thank you, Joseph, you knew exactly what I needed." She looked down at little Joseph and ran her fingers lovingly through his hair.

I, of course, hadn't known, but was glad she thought so! I had been more concerned that Joseph would start crying and wake up the whole household. Last night had been almost as difficult for Elizabeth and Zachariah as it was for us. Hopefully, they could sleep awhile longer. I sat there and watched Mary, admiring her. She caught me looking at her and said, "I must look terrible!"

"Well, you..." I began, but then smiled, "Dear, you always look wonderful to me." She laughed softly and looked down at baby Joseph. We both enjoyed the quietness and peace of the early morning.

When Joseph finished nursing, she started to get up, but I insisted she rest a while longer. There was no rush. "Mary, I think we should stay here for a few days, if Zachariah doesn't mind." She just nodded and, uncharacteristically, laid back down and went to sleep. For the first time in my life, I took care of all three boys while Mary slept.

When I took baby Joseph back to where the boys were sleeping, I laid down on the mat and played with him quietly. Then Jesus woke up and looked at me. "Good morning," I whispered.

Sometime later I woke up. I was alone. I jumped up, ashamed of myself—Where were the boys? I was supposed to be letting Mary sleep in! When I got to the dining room, there they were along with John, Elizabeth, and—to my chagrin—Mary.

"Well, it's about time, sleepyhead!" she said. But there was a twinkle in her eyes and a smile on her face.

I started to apologize, but Elizabeth interrupted, "Don't worry about it. She just got up herself. How about some porridge?" she added, as she handed Mary a steaming bowl.

After the boys finished eating, John jumped up and said to Jesus, "Let's go outside." John ran to the door and Jesus looked at me, eyes pleading to go.

Before I could answer, Elizabeth jumped in. "I don't know what John sees in that hillside, but he loves to go out there. Sometimes I think he'd spend all day there if we'd let him." Jesus nodded hopefully.

"I'm not too sure..." Mary said worriedly. Jesus' face fell.

"Please, Papa!" he pleaded.

"Well, I think..." I paused, winking at Jesus, at which he started jumping up and down. "I don't think..." teasing him a little, "I don't think it will be a problem." Then I added, "But don't be gone too long. We don't know when we're leaving for Nazareth." My voice trailed off as the boys bolted out the door. At the mention of Nazareth, the reality of last night's news came over us.

As the boys rushed out, they almost knocked over Zachariah, who was coming in the door. "They must be headed for the hills!" he exclaimed. After watching them for a moment, he turned back and noticed our sad faces.

"Would you like some good news?" he asked. We all nodded. "There's a caravan going toward Nazareth the day after tomorrow. That means you can stay here with us for a couple of days and then travel on in relative safety. Of course, you can stay here longer, if you wish."

Evidently he had risen early and gone into Jerusalem to see if he could find a caravan headed for Nazareth. "You're so gracious, Zachariah! Thank you. We'll go with the caravan and would love to stay here until then," I answered.

"Then that's settled," Elizabeth said as she put a bowl of porridge in front of me.

"Is there any more of that left?" Zachariah asked. Elizabeth nodded and went back to get another bowl. "You know," he said to Mary and me, "you kids really gave us a scare."

"How is that?" I wondered out loud.

"Well, when the two of you traveled to Bethlehem for the taxation, you didn't stop here on the way. Of course, we didn't know that at the time. But, later we got a message from Mary's parents, wondering if we had seen you. After a few months, we figured that the baby must have been born, but still didn't hear anything. I figured that at least we'd see you when you came to make the sacrifice offering, but we didn't. I couldn't send bad news to your family, so I didn't let them know. I decided that surely we'd see you at Passover feast, but we didn't—and then came the awful news about all the boy babies in Bethlehem being killed," Zechariah's voice broke as he continued. "There was no way I could keep that news from reaching Nazareth, so I began asking around trying to discover something about you. The only lead I got was from a young shepherd. But all he could tell me was that you had simply disappeared in the middle of the night."

"Josiah," Mary and I said in unison.

"Yes, I believe his name was Josiah. Well, your folks..."

Elizabeth came back with the porridge, but she had been listening and gave him a warning, "Zachariah, I don't think..."

He cut her off, "I think they ought to know. Nothing we can do will change what has already happened!" He stopped for a moment to take a bite.

"Please go on," Mary said, with tears in her eyes, "I want to know."

"I can tell you that your folks were heartbroken. There

was no way to console them. Not knowing troubled them the most—they could only think the worst. When winter came, they both got sick. Your mom died a few months later. We thought that your dad would pull through, but he didn't make it to springtime. That was last year." Zachariah paused, sighing, "It seemed like you had simply dropped off the face of the earth. We tried hard to find you, but no one could tell us anything."

When he paused again, I started to speak, but he held up his hand. "Let me tell you this, first," he said, then paused to gather his thoughts. "Just a few weeks ago I found this passage in the Scripture from the prophet Hosea:

> When Israel was a child, I loved him as a son, and I called my son out of Egypt.[18]

When I read that I began to wonder if you had gone to Egypt. We had not thought to look there."

"That's really in the Scripture?" I asked, incredulously, not expecting an answer.

The four of us sat there contemplating this revelation, while little Joseph slept and James played on the floor. Tears ran down Mary's cheeks. I knew she was hurting inside, realizing the pain we had inflicted on her parents. I felt

---

[18]Hosea 11:1

terrible, too, but knew there was nothing we could do now or could have done then.

"It may sound strange," I began, not knowing exactly what I was going to say, "but I'd like to praise God...for what He...has done in our lives. We have had the most incredible experiences and...He led us all the way." Mary nodded her head in agreement.

Then I told them our story from the beginning—the struggles in Bethlehem, the birth of our special son, the annunciation, the circumcision, the sacrifice offering, the visit of the kings, the angel's message—the whole story. By the time I finished we were all crying. Our tears were not only for the loss of Mary's parents, though that still hurt deeply, but for what we had seen—God at work—God's promised redemption of Israel.

I concluded, looking down at the floor, "Even after all these events for which I feel especially privileged, I've never really understood why God chose me, a poor carpenter to take part in this incredible story."

Zachariah responded immediately, "Oh, Joseph! You just told us that God spoke to you on four different occasions through an angel! You took the message on faith and acted on it each time! You never questioned! Compare that to what I did. I'm a priest. I commune with God for his people. I offer the sacrifices. I study the Scriptures daily. And when an angel visits me with a message from God, what did I do?" he asked, disgust in his voice. "My disbelieving heart prompted me to question the very God I serve! As soon as the words were out of my mouth, I knew I'd said the wrong thing. And because of my unbelief, I couldn't speak for nine months. It was only at John's circumcision, when his name was questioned and I wrote on a tablet, 'His name is John!' that God released my tongue."

Continuing in a calmer voice, Zachariah said, "By then I had stored up so many emotions, I could have praised God for hours! Fortunately, God's Spirit came over me and I began to prophesy about John...and Jesus who was yet to be born." Zachariah readjusted himself on the goatskin chair, then added, "However you may feel, Joseph, it is your humility, your humbleness that keeps you pliable and useful to God. Glory to His name!"

We were still sitting together when we heard John and Jesus coming back. Suddenly, we realized it was almost time for the evening meal. We had been sitting and talking most of the day!

Jesus came running in with a huge honey comb. "Mama! Papa! Look what John and I found!" When he noticed the tears in our eyes, his eagerness turned to alarm. "What's wrong?" he asked.

Mary and I both went to him and hugged him, honeycomb and all. We told him about his grandparents. As we explained what had happened, he began to cry. When we finished, he reached up and put his arms around Mary's neck. "I'm so sorry. I know you loved them very much. And I was looking forward to meeting them, too," he said in a broken voice. Then he kissed her.

Tears were flowing again, not only from Jesus, but from all of us. I was amazed at his perception of people and his care for them. Jesus hugged me next, then did the same to Elizabeth and Zachariah. When he got to John, he asked, "Did you ever meet my grandparents?"

"No," John responded, "but Mother told me all about them."

Jesus thought for a minute, then said, "But we'll all see them again...in heaven. Yes?"

"Yes, I believe you're right, Jesus," Zachariah replied.

At supper that evening, Zachariah brought out a scroll and read this Psalm:

May God be merciful and bless us.

May his face shine with favor upon us.

May your ways be known throughout the earth,

your saving power among people everywhere.

May the nations praise you, O God.

Yes, may all the nations praise you.

Let the whole world sing for joy,

because you govern them with justice

and direct the actions of the whole world.

May the nations praise you, O God.

Yes, may all the nations praise you.

Then the earth will yield its harvests,

and God, our God, will richly bless us.

Yes, God will bless us,

and people all over the world will fear him.[19]

By the time we left for Nazareth two days later, much healing had occurred in our hurting hearts. I knew the feeling of loss would surface again and again, especially when we got back to Nazareth, but the pain could no longer conquer us.

It was hard for Jesus and John to part. They had become great friends, even though they were so different. It was like seeing day and night walking around together! John could hardly stand still and loved adventure. Jesus was much calmer. Even though he was a little boy, he

---

[19]Psalm 67

seemed to spread sunshine in every situation. Living with him was a joy!

19

The New Home

Home at last! Our first night back in Nazareth we stayed in my small house with the carpentry shop. Since we arrived late in the day, we wanted to rest before facing Mary's parents' empty house. We hoped we could settle there. First, though, we needed to check with the other members of Mary's family. We were fairly sure none of them wanted to live in Nazareth. Mary said it had been hard enough to even get them to visit.

Since I had no family to look after my property, it was very dusty. But being so small, the five years of dust and cobwebs were easy to contend with. Surprisingly, everything in the little house was as I had left it—nothing had been stolen. What a blessing!

Before it got completely dark, Jesus and I went out to the old carpentry shop and checked the work benches and heavier tools that I had left behind. "Tomorrow we'll clean this up," I told Jesus, "so we can start to work."

He looked at me, puzzled. "Do you already have jobs to do?"

"Oh, nothing that pays. But if we stay here, we'll need to add some rooms. And if we do go to your mother's house, there will be many things to fix and furniture to build."

"Papa, do you want to live at mother's house?"

"It would be nice. There would certainly be more room for us. I could keep the carpentry shop here so that when I went home in the evening I'd leave the shop and all its problems. Yes, it would be nice."

The next morning we got up early—excited to visit the other house and see what it was like. Fortunately, we didn't have far to walk. And, we didn't have to carry anything— except Joseph. Even James toddled along most of the way, holding Jesus' hand.

As we walked, the memories flooded in—of all the times I had walked this road. Mary was quiet, as well, and I wondered if she could handle seeing her old house without her parents. *It will be hard for both of us to be in their house without their cheerful presence,* I mused.

Mary's voice interrupted my thoughts, "Joseph, I'm really excited about seeing the old house. There'll be plenty of room for all of us—Mom and Dad had a big family there." She paused, looked up at me with a trembling smile, then added, "I know I'll miss Mom and Dad, but it's okay. The time with Elizabeth and Zachariah was a great blessing. The Lord has taken the pain out from my heart."

At that moment we turned the corner onto her old street. We stopped and stared at the house. It looked the same as I remembered it. Whitewashed walls, thatched roof, and rickety fence that circled the yard. It really looked nice—too nice! Too neat to have been empty for the past year. "It looks like some...," I began, when Mary interrupted me.

"Who could be living here?" She paused as I shook my head. We stood there like we were rooted to the ground.

Jesus tugged at my hand, "Is that our new house?"

"We thought it was, but now I'm not too sure." I stopped for a moment, not sure what to do. Finally, I said, "Let's go and find out!"

At the gate, we stopped. "Shalom, anybody home?" I called.

Suddenly, we heard noises in the house and a man's face popped out the window. He said, "Well, look at the beggars!" then turned back to someone inside and said, "Can you believe it, beggars at this hour of the morning!"

When a female voice answered, "Who is it, Abner?" I heard Mary gasp! Before I could look at her, Abner yelled out the window, "How should I know? I don't know any beggars!" He spat the word out like it hurt his teeth to say it.

I looked at Mary. She was as white as a sheet. As I took little Joseph from her—before she dropped him—she whispered, "Elizabeth and Abner!" I looked at her, puzzled. "My sister, named after our cousin, and her husband Abner. When she left here to marry Abner she vowed she'd never come back."

Before I could comprehend the situation, the woman appeared at the door. "Those aren't normal beggars. That's my sister Mary!" Now that she had our full attention, she shouted, "Murderers, murderers!" and spat on the ground. Then she noticed the children and added, "Little murderers, too!"

James was the first to react. "Mommy, I'm hungry!" he whined.

Mary quieted him down, straightened her shoulders and said, "Elizabeth, what do you mean? We're not murderers. Who do you think we murdered?"

"You really don't know, do you? Well, MY parents are dead because of you!" How could she say such a thing. They were Mary's parents, too. But she wasn't through, "Yeah, first they thought your darling, precious, SPECIAL baby was killed in Bethlehem where you ran off to. Then when you turned up missing, they couldn't imagine what had happened. I know what happened. You're no better than me!" She paused for a moment. We stood there dumbfounded, then she turned to Abner and said, "You know, Abner, I bet they were coming here to take over this house. Now that they killed my parents they must have figured they could live here. HA! Over my dead body."

Abner had a smirk on his face. As he pulled his silken robe a little more closely over his more than ample body, he said disdainfully, "Our poor relations! What a pity they showed up. I was just beginning to enjoy Nazareth."

Shocked into silence by their outburst and

accusations, I finally found my voice. "I'm sorry we disturbed you so early in the morning," I said calmly. "You are partly right. We did come here thinking we might live here, but..." I couldn't finish.

Elizabeth hissed, "You better believe you're not going to live here!"

As I took Mary's hand and started to leave, I heard Abner say to Elizabeth, "Well, at least they didn't make a scene."

Shoulders slumped, we dragged our feet back the way we had come. As we walked away, Jesus pulled on my tunic. "She wasn't very nice, was she, Papa? She didn't even have tears in her eyes when she talked about her parents being dead," he said in disbelief.

"She was talking about your mother's parents, too, son!"

"You mean Grandmother and Grandfather?" When he saw me nodding, he went on plaintively, "But you didn't cause them to die. Uncle Zachariah said..."

Suddenly, Mary found her voice, "Oh Joseph, I'm so sorry! I forgot all about Elizabeth and Abner." She began sobbing. Jesus went to her, took her hand, hugged it to his cheek, and held it there while we walked. Though she could barely talk through her tears and grief, Mary began to tell us about Elizabeth.

It seems that Elizabeth, who was five years older than Mary, had enjoyed being the baby of the family. When Mary came along and stole her position, Elizabeth rejected her. From the moment Mary was born, she would have nothing to do with her. The aloofness between them continued through their childhood years. But when Elizabeth became a teenager, her aloofness turned to animosity and their relationship worsened. Finally, Elizabeth ran away and married Abner and Mary hadn't seen her since.

By the time we got back to the carpentry shop, our emotions had settled down. Jesus skipped down the path ahead of us, while I thought seriously about how to expand the living quarters of my house and shop. I had already thought of a simple plan that might work. It wouldn't be fancy, but would give us the space we needed fairly quickly.

Before we sat down to eat, that evening—the beginning of a new day for us—I quoted a Psalm of praise to our God. In my prayer, I thanked God for what had happened: "Lord, you made me humble. It would have been difficult to be humble in a big house." When I opened my eyes, I looked into Mary's which were moist, but bright. There was an approving smile on her face. *You're right. We don't need a big house*, her eyes seemed to say.

As we ate in peace, I wondered about Elizabeth and Abner. Were they at peace? Were they guilty of the very things she had accused us of? Then I remembered James and our enduring relationship—I couldn't wait to see my old friend, the one I had named my first son for. At least I had one great friend!

20

The Friendship

We worked hard over the next several days. While Mary was settling and arranging our few pieces of furniture, I was adding a small room so that in the evenings, after the boys were in bed, Mary and I would have a place to sit and talk.

The last bit of money from the kings was spent on that new room. As soon as it was done, I would need to get some work that paid so we could continue to eat.

Mary and I rarely left the house except to get water or purchase a few items of food, but when we did venture out nothing unusual happened. Mary said that some of the women at the well looked at her strangely. However, since she knew most of them, she always spoke to them. A few were friendly. Looking back, it was a bit strange since—before we left Nazareth five years ago—Mary was well-known and liked in the village. We guessed that Elizabeth and Abner had been talking, putting a question mark about us in people's minds.

After we'd been back about a week, I was just starting the framework for the addition when I looked up and saw my friend James coming down the road. He was leading a donkey loaded with supplies. When I saw him, I called out to Mary, "Guess who's coming our way?"

I climbed down to wash up. I had been looking forward to seeing James, but was a little ashamed I hadn't been over to his house already. I was anxious to tell him all about Jehu and what a great a donkey he was, even though, I had been skeptical about his praises.

I finished washing up and got to the door just as he stopped. "James, my friend! Shalom, brother!" We embraced, holding each other as only close friends do.

His first words surprised me a little, "So you're back in Nazareth! I'd heard rumors you'd returned." His voice sounded hesitant, like he had heard some other, not so good, rumors.

"Yes, we're back home," I replied. "I have been dying to get over to see you, but had to get going on this extra room. We've been on the road for so long with no place to call our own that I had to do this first—for Mary and the children."

"You could have called on me. I would have come over and helped." There was hurt in his voice. He went over to inspect my work, while I looked at the load of materials he had on his donkey—just the things I needed to finish the roof.

As I followed him to the new addition I asked, "How are Abigail and the girls—is it still just girls?"

"Yes, all girls—they're fine. They've grown a lot since you last saw them. It's been about five years...when we did the roof on my house."

He paused for a moment still looking over the work I'd done. Then in a strained voce, he told me, "You know, Joseph, we've been worried about you. You were gone for so long—we never heard from you—Mary's folks were upset beyond belief when they heard about the slaughter in Bethlehem. I never understood that, but I guess they figured you and Mary had a baby boy by then. They tried to get some word about you, but only found that you had left Bethlehem in the middle of the night."

He looked me squarely in the eyes and went on, "What's happened to you, Joseph? That's not the Joseph I knew. You were always so...so careful. I never saw you act like this until you left for Bethlehem on such short notice. What's happened to you?"

What should I tell him? Do I start at the beginning with the angel visiting me? No, he'd just laugh. James was a good man, but not one to accept a story like that without a lot of explaining. Nor did I want to tell him that Jesus was God's son. No, that was God's duty. I took a deep breath and was about to launch into some explanation when James stopped me.

"Mary! You look wonderful! Now, who is that in your arms?" He turned around to me excitedly, expectantly.

I looked at James' expectant face and said, "Oh, this is baby Joseph." As I said the name, his face changed suddenly. He must have expected me to say James, not Joseph. Evidently he didn't see the two boys hiding behind Mary's robe. Before I could explain, Jesus suddenly appeared in front of Mary. He was smiling like a donkey with a mouthful of oats.

James breathed a sigh of relief and said with a smile, "So this is J..."

But I broke in, laughing, "This is Jesus!"

He stopped smiling, "He's at least five years old! You can't have an older son!"

"No, but," Mary said as she released James, "this is James, your namesake!"

He looked from one of us to the other, disbelief written all over his face. Finally, with hurt in his voice, he said, "You *were* my best friend! You promised me you'd name your FIRST son after me!" He turned away, adding, "I suppose some of those rumors I heard are true. You should have been named Jacob instead of Joseph." And with that he stormed out. Grabbing his donkey's reins and hitting him with a stick, he left hurriedly, not looking back.

Only once before had I felt so utterly helpless. My best friend rejected me, just because I didn't name my first son—or who he thought was *my* first son—after him. *The jokester couldn't take a joke himself, could he?* Mary tried to console me, but I couldn't get over it. Jesus came over after I sat down, crawled up in my lap, put his arms around my neck and held me.

The two of us sat there for a long time as I thought about my friend James. He must have been deadly serious about a promise I had made lightly. But what else could I do? There had been no way to tell him before we left that Mary was already pregnant. He might have been the first to throw stones, friend or not. And with our decision to let God, not us, announce His son, I couldn't explain things to James—at least not fully. Besides, he didn't give me a chance.

"Oh James, James, how I want to tell you all that God has done in my life," I whispered under my breath. But would he receive that message? I didn't know. Maybe it would only reinforce the malicious rumors he had heard. I prayed, "Oh, God! My best friend! Help me, Lord! I can't handle this!" Mary finally called Jesus to help her with the evening meal.

In my desperation, I continued to pray. In the quietness —dear Mary was keeping the boys out of my way—I realized that God must feel something like this when men reject Him or don't let Him speak. And God loves His people much more than I loved James! My pain was nothing compared to His.

The sun was almost down when Jesus came to get me for the evening meal. As I looked into his eyes, I could see the concern he had for me. How could a child of five show such love for his father? *His eyes seemed say, I love you, Father, even if your best friend left you, I still love you.* Then he took my hand and we walked hand in hand to the dinner table.

Everyone was quiet and sober. Normally when I prayed, I looked up toward heaven, but tonight, humbled, I bowed my head. Instead of beginning with a Psalm, I spoke to God, personally, "Father in heaven, great is your name! Tonight my heart is breaking for my friend James. But you have shown me today how your heart must grieve when your people fail to listen to you, fail to trust you, fail to love you unconditionally. My heart is hurting now, not because I lost a friend, but because James doesn't understand. But I'll wait on you—when the right time comes, bring him back so I can share your great love with him. Until then...," I paused for a moment, lifted my head, then said loudly, "Until then,

Praise the LORD!

Praise God in his sanctuary;

praise him in his mighty heaven!

Praise him for his mighty works;

praise his unequaled greatness!

Praise him with a blast of the ram's horn;

praise him with the lyre and harp!

Praise him with the tambourine and dancing;

praise him with strings and flutes!

Praise him with a clash of cymbals;

praise him with loud clanging cymbals.

Let everything that breathes

sing praises to the LORD!

Praise the LORD!"[20]

By the time I finished my plate was full—full of tears. Mary jumped up, got a towel and dried it off. Pulling myself together, I looked around the table at the boys God had given me—Jesus was smiling again and James was mischievously reaching out to get a piece of bread before he was served. Baby Joseph wrapped up tightly, was sleeping peacefully. "Thank you, Mary!" I breathed.

"Thank you, Joseph! I know that James will come back

---

[20]Psalm 150:1-6

to you."

I agreed, but neither of us guessed how long it would take.

21

The Furniture

After a while, life in Nazareth became more normal. Most folks were beginning to accept us as regular people. The rumors and tales subsided, but the estrangement between Mary and her sister continued. Abner? Well, he had become a big man in the village. People looked up to him because of his prosperity.

We had been back in Nazareth a couple of years when I ran into Abner one day outside the village. I was surprised when he asked me to make some furniture for their home. I didn't know what to say. Even though it would mean some extra shekels for us, I didn't want the job. Abner's reputation was well known. I knew that if he found anything wrong with the pieces I made for him, he'd never let me forget it. He saw my reluctance, but wouldn't take 'no' for an answer. Finally, I gave him a price that was more than double what I would normally have charged. "That's highway robbery," he roared almost ripping his silken robe in disgust. After a bit of haggling he agreed to a price somewhere between the one I first quoted and my normal price. I should have been pleased, but I didn't feel good about the deal.

Then Abner said, "You're a good man, Joseph!" He sounded proud of himself for getting the price down and I smiled weakly, until he continued: "But, there's one other thing you have to do for me. You can't tell anyone who you're making this for." My smile turned into a troubled frown. When he saw my face, he began casting about for words: "It's a secret...ah, it's a surprise, yes that's right, it's a surprise for Elizabeth and I don't want her to find out about it." I wasn't happy about this. I'd had enough intrigue in my life already. But since I had agreed to make the furniture, there was nothing else I could do. He gave me the deposit I needed to purchase the materials and we parted.

As he walked away, he had a proud swagger that said he had gotten the best end of the deal. I returned home, heavy of heart, wondering what he had up his sleeve. *Why didn't I stand by my initial refusal?* I fretted. However, we really needed the income and he probably knew that.

Jesus was becoming a good carpenter. He still had many things to learn, but by the time he was seven, he was working regularly with me in the shop. He asked questions about everything and I shared everything I knew. It was a training time, the same way I had learned the trade from my father.

James helped out a little by now, too, but we didn't really get a lot of work out of him. He was almost five years old when we began making Abner's furniture. It was his job to clean up the sawdust and shavings. Sometimes when Jesus or I couldn't find a tool we needed, the search would begin. When we finally found it covered up with shavings, James would laugh like it was all a big joke. We would laugh with him and then get back to work.

Jesus probably taught James as much about carpentry as I did. He was more patient than I was, and certainly better at explaining and answering all the 'whys' James came up with.

All three of us bent our backs to the task of making Abner's furniture, a job that would take several months. I hoped to finish it before we took our annual pilgrimage to Jerusalem. But there was one problem. Abner wanted me to keep the individual pieces until the whole set was completed and as the work progressed, our shop became more and more crowded. We hardly had space to work! However, we managed by making the bigger pieces first and stacking the smaller ones on top. At least, this way, we could still move around.

Finally, we finished and I contacted Abner. Instead of being excited that the furniture was done, he seemed almost uninterested. He said he would have to come and inspect the furniture first, but he didn't have time just now. I took a deep breath and plunged in: "Abner, I know that you are not religious so you may not realize that we go to Jerusalem every year at this time. I've completed the job. You can pick it up now or you can leave it, but there will be no one at our house for more than two weeks." Despite the frown on his face, I continued, "There's not enough room inside my house for the furniture, so it will be left outside in the shop. Since everyone knows we will be gone, I cannot be responsible for it. Besides, I'd like to be paid so we can make the trip."

He finally agreed, but not without a lot of mumbling and muttering under his beard about me charging him too much in the first place, about the inconvenience of getting it now, and other imagined grievances. While he was getting the shekels together, I waited patiently, trying to ignore his complaints. After handing me the money, he said he would have someone pick it all up on the morrow. Then he added, "Now, Joseph, you swear that it is all just like I ordered?"

"I don't swear, but I think you'll find it satisfactory," I replied.

"Well, I still think you charged me too much, but I suppose I owe it to Elizabeth to do something nice for her," he blustered, his voice trailing off. Then he added, "Remember now, you can't tell anyone that you made this furniture for me!"

I nodded and left. Little did he realize that my furniture had a distinctive style. Anyone who had seen my work would be able to recognize it. However, since Elizabeth seldom ventured out to other people's homes, I figured it would be a long time before she discovered who made her new furniture. But I had more important things on my mind now—the annual trip to Jerusalem.

The next day, a man arrived with a cart pulled by a donkey and we loaded the furniture. He was taking great pains to tie everything down, carefully, like he was taking it to Jerusalem or beyond. Finally, my curiosity got the best of me and I asked why he was being so careful since he only had to go only a short distance.

"I'll give you two reasons." he said. "First, I'm getting this for Abner and if there is a scratch on it he'll blame me and refuse to pay me. Second, I'm not going just a short distance. I was instructed to ride way out of town, making sure that everything gets dusty, and get to his house late this afternoon. Don't ask me why." He shrugged his shoulders and went back to loading the cart.

As he left with the furniture, I shook my head. I was sure Abner's story to Elizabeth would be that he found the furniture in another town and had it brought to Nazareth. I also had a strong feeling that this was not the last we would hear about this!

22

The Temple

The yearly trip to Jerusalem was a high point in our lives. We probably looked forward to it more than most. I guess that after spending so many years of traveling, being settled in a little village like Nazareth was just a little confining. We always enjoyed the trip—visiting with fellow travelers and the carefree time with our kids. But there was another, more important reason.

It became our tradition to embark on the journey with the first group of pilgrims. But instead of going directly to Jerusalem, we would veer off to the hill country and spend a few days with Zachariah and Elizabeth. The children enjoyed exploring the hillsides with John, seeing all kinds of things they had never seen before. And Mary loved being with Elizabeth, the only person with whom she could speak freely.

Each year, after the first trip into the hillside with the other children, Jesus would gravitate to Zachariah. They would spend hours discussing the Scriptures. Jesus asked questions and Zachariah answered. Zachariah usually had some of the scrolls on hand—older copies that were no longer used in the temple, he said. However I think he brought them home before we arrived anticipating the study time with Jesus. They would pore over the texts all day long. Jesus seemed to absorb everything and continuously asked probing questions. Sometimes I joined in and was welcome to do so, but I seldom had anything to contribute. Usually, I just listened and reflected on the things they were talking about in relation to my experiences. But when they began discussing some of the finer points of the law, I would wander off to visit with Mary and Elizabeth.

At the last possible moment, we would leave for Jerusalem and make it just in time for the Passover feast. While in Jerusalem, I would look for a group that was staying a little longer and make arrangements to travel back to Nazareth with them. Then, as soon as we could, we would leave and return to Zachariah's home for another heavenly two days or so with him and Elizabeth.

On the journey home, Jesus and I would discuss the things he had learned. Sometimes James listened in. He seemed awed at how much Scripture Jesus could quote and discuss. It was about the only time James was quiet. As he listened, I prayed that what he heard would someday bear fruit in his life.

We enjoyed this yearly feast for six years but the year Jesus turned twelve, we received news, that Zachariah had passed away. We left for Jerusalem early that year, thinking we might be a comfort to Elizabeth. But we weren't.

Elizabeth was in another world. She barely talked. The only time she opened up was to express her fear of what would happen to John. She was quite old and afraid that she, too, would die before John was grown. Even when I reminded her that my parents had died while I was still young, she was not comforted. Finally, we realized there was nothing we could do to help Elizabeth. So, leaving her in the care of her servants, we sadly said our good-byes and headed for Jerusalem, knowing that we would not be coming back after the feast. Maybe next year.

I remember little about the feast time that year. Both Mary and I had other things on our minds. Mary was concerned about Elizabeth and I was thinking about the loss of the one man with whom I could talk freely about Jesus. Now I thought of hundreds of questions I should have asked Zachariah about the Messiah, but didn't. With heavy hearts and minds, we went through the motions of the Passover feast without really participating.

After the Feast was over, we began the journey back to Nazareth, this time with friends instead of strangers. Actually I was surprised at how enjoyable the trip was! Even James, my old friend, joked with us, though his jokes did have a little bite in them. He said things like, "So Jacob...er, Joseph, you've condescended to go back to Nazareth with us common folks, huh?" Everybody laughed good-naturedly and, as there wasn't much I could say, I just smiled and nodded my head. In a small way, it felt good that he had actually spoken to me. The spirit of the group was congenial and we had a great time, even though I missed the deep conversations Jesus and I had on other trips. Then I realized I hadn't seen Jesus for awhile. *He must be walking with the other children*, I thought.

But he wasn't. When we stopped for the evening, we couldn't find Jesus anywhere. No one—not even the children —remembered seeing or talking to him on the whole trip. Mary was beside herself, but I tried to stay calm, at least outwardly. I reminded Mary that Jesus was not irresponsible.

"He was probably talking to someone and forgot the time. He's made this trip many times before so he knows the way. No doubt he's with another group by now, headed this way." But in my heart I, too, was worried.

We had no choice but to stay with the group. It was too dangerous to travel at night, especially for two people traveling alone. We didn't sleep very much. My thoughts were jumbled. *This is God's special son. Would He allow something to happen to him before he accomplished the purpose he came here for? I know God wants to redeem His people, but how will that happen? What part will Jesus play? Jesus and Zachariah discussed this a lot. On the other hand, God has entrusted Jesus into our hands and he expects us to protect and care for him. I'm sure God isn't pleased we left Jerusalem without Jesus. But...* For hours my mind flip-flopped between these questions and thoughts until, finally, I fell asleep.

Early the next morning, Mary shook me awake. Now that was a shock! I couldn't remember the last time someone woke *me* up! "Quickly, Joseph, we need to get on the way! Jesus could be in danger!" I wasn't going to argue with her. She might be right, though I didn't really think so. I did know that we needed to make arrangements for our other children so we could travel back to Jerusalem more quickly. I decided to take a chance on James.

My old friend was up preparing breakfast—he was unusual that way. It reminded me of our trips to Jerusalem before I was married. I always traveled with James and his family in those days. Every morning, he was the first one up, even before me, so he could fix breakfast. He didn't do this at home—only when the family traveled.

"Good morning, James." He just nodded. "I have a problem..."

"I know," he said with a little animosity in his voice, "what do you want me to do?"

I waited, trying to put the words together in the right order: "Uh, I'd like for you to keep my James, your namesake, for us while Mary and I return to Jerusalem. I know you've been upset with me for many years now, but I just can't explain all that, especially at the moment and right now...I really need your help."

He looked up at me, eyes sparkling. I knew he had some joke he wanted to spout out, but he refrained himself and said, "Ok, I suppose second place is better than no place at all. Send him over. We'll see what he's made of."

"Thanks, James." And I left before he could change his mind.

In the meantime, Mary passed little Joseph off to another family who also had an eight-year-old.

It took us little more than half a day to travel back to Jerusalem. When we arrived we immediately began searching. First of all, we went to the inn we had stayed in during the feast. Unfortunately, no one at the inn had seen Jesus; yes, they remembered him, but had not seen him since we left. Before we left the inn, I secured a room, knowing that—even if we found Jesus right away—we would have to stay overnight.

Our next hope was some of the other inns where friends had stayed. But in every place we received the same response, "No, we haven't seen him."

After dark we returned to our lodgings. We were too late for the evening meal, but that wasn't a problem. Neither of us was hungry. That evening we made careful plans for searching the city. Feverishly, we planned every detail, trying not to miss any place we could think of that Jesus might have gone. We prayed together—prayed fervently that God would lead us to our boy.

Still, Mary was not just a little upset with me when I went to bed. "How can you sleep at a time like this? Don't you have any concern at all?" she cried out.

I had to bite my tongue not to respond in kind and, after

a moment, said, "Yes, I am very concerned, but I know two things. If I don't get some rest, I'll not be fully functional tomorrow. And, while I'm concerned, I'm not really worried. We'll find Jesus. God will protect him." And with that I turned over to go to sleep. Actually, it took a while, but I knew that if we continued our verbal battle one of us would get mad and I knew it would probably be me!

The next morning, full of expectations, we set out on our search, but by mid-day even I was beginning to worry. We returned to the inn, dispirited, disheveled, but not quite defeated. *Where could Jesus possibly be?*

We ate a little food and rested. Neither of us had the energy to think, plan, or even to argue. But I could pray, and did. "Father, we don't know what to do. I know you have some plan in this, but we don't know which way to turn. Please give us direction. We are trusting you. Amen."

After a little bit, an idea came to me and I told Mary, "As far as I can tell, the only place we have not looked is the Temple. Let's go there!" Though her look said, "Why there?" she was the first one out the door!

When we reached the Temple we saw no one. Everything was quiet. I suppose that after a week of intense activity, the temple workers were taking a break. We stopped, somewhat awed by the quietness—it was so unlike the temple we knew that echoed with the sounds of the Passover services—so different from the noises of the merchandise sellers along the way.

As we stood there, gradually adjusting to the stillness, we suddenly heard voices. Before we could discover the direction they came from, all was quiet again. We moved further into the Temple building. As we neared the other side, we heard the voices again—four or five men talking at once. We quickly followed the sound.

Looking into the room, we saw teachers and scribes and doctors of the law all talking and gesturing earnestly. It must be an important meeting, I thought. I was trying to decide if I should interrupt them, when I heard a familiar voice. Relief flooded my spirit. We had found Jesus!

And I should have known! I remembered the discussions he had with Zachariah. It seemed so natural. This was exactly what we had done every year for the past six years, both before and after the Passover. Of course we were surprised that he was in the temple, but not so surprised that the teachers who were talking to him seemed amazed at his understanding and his answers.

Mary ran into the room and said, "Son! Why have you done this to us? Your father and I have been frantic, searching for you everywhere."[21]

"But why did you need to search?" he calmly asked. "Didn't you know that I must be in my Father's house?"[22]

"Excuse us," I said to the men, "but we've been looking for this young man for three days." They looked puzzled. Evidently they were so amazed at what they heard from Jesus they were not even aware of how long they had been talking. Nevertheless, they seemed to be waiting for some explanation so—not knowing whether it made any sense or not—I added, "He and his Uncle Zachariah used to spend a few days after the Feast talking about the Scriptures."

"Oh, Zachariah was his uncle? Now there was a godly man!" one of them said as the others nodded in agreement. Another added, "We miss him around here." As we were leaving, another called out, "Come back again, young man, we'd like to talk to you again." We nodded as we left.

It was too late to travel so we went back to the inn, had our evening meal, and talked with Jesus about his experiences in the Temple. It was such a relief to have him back with us that neither of us had the heart to scold him. Also unasked and, of course, unanswered, was what he meant by *expecting*

---

[21]Luke 2:48

[22]Luke 2:49

that we should know that he would be in his "Father's house?"

We went to bed early that night, slept soundly, and got up at daybreak to begin the journey home. Now that Jesus was with us, Mary became so worried about the other children that there was no resting along the way. It was walk, walk, walk, from before daybreak until it was almost too late to find a safe place to stay for the night. The pace that Mary's concern forced on us left us no breath for talking and, by the time we got settled in that evening, we were too tired to talk. Jesus never complained. He walked. He helped. And he smiled. Me? I was beginning to lose my smile.

We caught up with James and the group just before they got to Nazareth. When I went to collect my James, I could see they were having a great time. For sure, they weren't all tired out like I was. We passed a few pleasantries and then James asked, "Where'd you find him?"

"In the Temple," I said matter-of-factly.

"In the Temple?" he exploded, "What in the world was he doing in the Temple? We just spent a week in and out of the Temple. Why in the world would he want to stay in the Temple?"

"I really cannot answer why, but he was there talking to the teachers and scribes," I explained.

"Talking to the teachers! Yea, I bet he was. You know,

Joseph, I think you better watch that kid," he said, shaking his head. "He may be getting too religious on you. You'll never get one of my daughters to marry him if he's too religious. No, sireee!"

I was dumbfounded by his words, but could offer no response. So I didn't try.

Just before we parted, as James was handing his namesake to me, my old friend came the closest to an apology I had ever heard from him. He said, "Now, this little fellow—he's a pretty good kid. Aren't you James?" They were both grinning.

"Bye, Uncle James," little James called as he turned back and waved.

"Bye to you and come over to see me sometime if you can get your father to let you out of that sweat shop of his." He winked at us, waved his hand, turned around and poked one of his daughters in the ribs. She jumped and said disdainfully, "Oh, Papa!"

We went home, happy to be together again. It was going to feel so good to get back to our home and our normal routine.

23

The Young Man

Normalcy did come and continued for years. Our family grew—as did the carpentry business—in about equal proportions. So we still struggled to make ends meet. Every year we made the trek to Jerusalem, but it was never as exciting as before when we could visit Zachariah and Elizabeth. Jesus never stayed behind and talked to the priests and teachers again. Instead, he would attend all the Passover services listening intently. Sometimes he frowned when he heard something he didn't agree with, but he never rebuked his elders. He only responded when he was specifically asked a question. Then he would give a simple, direct answer. This brought him great favor with the teachers. I learned from James that this was also true when they went to classes at the synagogue in Nazareth. Even he realized that Jesus often knew more than the teachers. However, Jesus did not push himself on anyone.

Another of Jesus' habits was to gather the children around him and teach them. Actually he didn't have to do much gathering—they usually flocked around him anyhow! Occasionally, an adult or two would be in the group and they would comment to me how well Jesus knew the Scriptures. Looking back, I can see how carefully he remained true to himself and yet, held himself back. While I wanted him to be more active and teach more, I got the impression that it was not yet God's time for him. This was a difficult lesson for me in the beginning, since I wanted so badly for people to understand who he really was. But God was waiting, and so was Jesus.

Jesus was an exceptionally good carpenter. Our little shop began to gain a reputation for turning out excellent work for a low price. According to Abner, charging too little was a big mistake—except, of course, when we'd made things for him!

Jesus was much more sensitive to people and their

needs than I ever was. For example, one morning, just after breakfast, he went out and picked up a new plough we had made, put it on his back and started down the road. I called after him, "Wait a minute, Jesus! Who did you sell the plough to?"

"I didn't," he answered, "I heard that Jacob on the other side of town broke his yesterday trying to get a new field ready for planting. I thought he could use it." He paused, looking at me intently, "Do you want to come along?"

"Y...Yes, just a minute. I'll be there directly." After giving James, Joseph, and Simon some jobs to do around the shop, I took off. When I caught up with Jesus, I ventured, "Do you remember that we made that plough with the idea of generating some extra cash?"

"Yes, I know that, Father, but Jacob is in real need," he replied. "I had heard about his plan to open up that new field last year, but then he got sick and couldn't work. He really needs that field for his wheat."

I had planned to use the money from the sale of that plough to do something special for Jesus since he worked so hard in the shop. But I didn't want to tell him that.

Jesus continued, "Besides, I'll get Jacob's old plough and repair it. Then we can either sell it, or perhaps Jacob will return the new plough and get his old one back when he can."

He paused, "However it works out, God will supply our needs."

From the view of compassion, I couldn't fault Jesus on his logic so I replied weakly, "I see." We walked on in silence.

When we arrived at Jacob's house and he saw Jesus with the new plough, tears welled up in his eyes. "Oh, Joseph!" he said, "T'is truly a gift from God!" Suddenly, I realized just how true that was, and could not respond. Jesus didn't say a word. He set down the new plough, picked up the old broken one, and we started back home. Jacob continued to thank us profusely as we went out the gate. Jesus simply said, "Success with the new field!" I had hoped Jesus would make some deal with Jacob concerning the return of the plough. But he didn't. So far as Jesus was concerned, he had just given away our new plough with no expectation for its return. And Jacob had received a gift from God, literally!

After I regained my composure, I said to Jesus, "Thank you, son, I needed that."

He said, "Just a cup of cool water."

And so Jesus found favor in everyone's eyes— everyone except his own brothers. There were two reasons for this. One was that Mary doted on him, serving him first and giving him anything he asked for—which wasn't much since he asked for little. But to his brothers, this was favoritism. They failed to realize that there was a big difference in their wants and what Jesus asked for. The other problem was that, too often, Mary said things like, "Why can't you be more like Jesus?" I talked to her about this many times, but each time she would look at me with hurt in her eyes. Jesus was her special son.

Jesus never returned the spitefulness of his brothers. In reality, they had no reason to complain. Jesus was always kind to them, but they often took advantage of him and his kindness. His sisters never had a problem with Jesus. The same was true of Judas, his youngest brother, who was too young to be jealous, as were the two youngest sisters.

I wished, hoped, and prayed that this tension in the family would go away, but as the boys grew older, the situation grew even more tense. Mary and I had agreed that we wouldn't tell the children about the special birth of Jesus. We still believed that this was God's responsibility—in His time He would let it be known. And, if we did tell them—well, who knows the stories the boys might tell their friends in spite. We didn't need the uproar it could cause! Especially now that we had some peace with the community.

I wanted to learn more from Jesus. Mary and I knew in our hearts that he was or would be the Messiah. Like all Jews, we longed for a conqueror to emancipate our people from the Romans. And here he was—living in our house! Yes, it was difficult knowing who Jesus was and keeping quiet about it.

Several times when Jesus and I were working in the shop without the other boys, I'd bring up the future. One time I asked him, "Jesus, I know that you are God's Son. Your birth was miraculous. I know that you will be Messiah, but when will this happen? I so want to get out of this oppression under the Romans!"

"That's up to the Heavenly Father. It's not in my hands," he quietly replied, never missing a beat in his work.

His response showed me he already knew something it had taken me most of my life to learn: Our Father works on a different time schedule than we humans.

Nevertheless, I tried again. "Jesus, if I knew what you know and could relate to people the way you do, I'd be fighting like Jehu under a heavy load. I'd be anxious to get moving!"

He looked at me and smiled, probably picturing our old donkey struggling to pull the loaded cart. We always had to push to help him get it started. "Don't push me, like you do Jehu, Father," he said. "Our Heavenly Father knows what is best." He paused a moment and added, "In some ways I am anxious to move on, but it will not be all glory, as you may wish. There will be difficulties, even suffering before the glory days come. And yet..." His voice trailed off and a far away look came into his moist eyes. "And yet," he began again, "there will be peace at the same time."

"You're right. I was pushing," I admitted. "I'll try to be patient, though that's not my best trait!"

When he looked up his eyes were clear, his face resolute, "Yes, patience may not be your strength, but you have other strengths, Father, like trust and love and faithfulness, qualities that more than compensate."

I frowned, thinking only of my failures. He continued, "For example you trusted by faith that my birth was of the Holy Spirit. You loved your bride-to-be in spite of the possible consequences. You have been faithful to God who gave you the difficult task of staying in the background." He moved around the work bench, "And you have been a wonderful father and teacher to me. More than that, you are an example of all the things you taught. I love you, Father!" And with that he embraced me. "Yes, I love you."

It was a holy moment, and yet, bitter sweet.

208

24

The Return

By the time Jesus was in his twenties, the Joseph of Nazareth family was accepted as honorable, upstanding citizens by everyone. Everyone, that is, except Mary's sister Elizabeth. Even her husband Abner had accepted us, although we didn't see him often.

One day I met Abner in town. As we were talking, I happened to mention the furniture and asked if it was wearing well. He said, "Oh, it's great! You know, Elizabeth has been bugging me for years about who made that furniture, but I've always just told her that I picked it up on one of my trips. She never really believed it. The other night she brought it up again," he stopped, shaking his head and then continued. "I was so tired of hearing the question over and over again that I finally told her you made it. She turned every color in the rainbow! She fussed and fumed, cried and swore til I wondered if she was going to lose her mind! So I said, 'Hey, do you want me to get rid of the stuff?' She looked at me with her swollen eyes, shook her head, and started crying some more. The problem is she's bragged so much to everyone she knows about how beautiful and great that furniture is, that if she were to get rid of it now she'd never be able to face her friends. Actually, I wish she had said yes. I could sell the furniture for twice what I paid you!" He laughed.

It was difficult for me to understand why Elizabeth hated us so...how she could continue to snub her sister and tell untrue stories about our family. Fortunately, few people really believed her anymore. From the beginning, most of Nazareth knew who had made the furniture. That she bragged about it kept them laughing behind her back.

I'll never forget that particular spring and summer. Our eighth child, Ruth, was born in the spring. My quiver was full and I felt blessed. Even though the oppression from the Romans was great, there was peace between us and the community. James and his family came over several times for evening fellowship and we sometimes went to his house. These were really great times since the children played so well together.

Following that glorious summer, the weather turned cold early and stayed cold. Although there was no heat in the carpentry shop, there was work to be done and we had to endure it. I was getting older, but no one could persuade me to take it easier. Stubbornly I continued my work in the cold shop.

About the middle of winter, my joints started aching and it was difficult to get up in the mornings. I struggled along until, one day, I collapsed in the shop and Jesus had to carry me to my bed. Even though it was cold, I felt hot and was sweating like an overloaded donkey. I stayed in bed the rest of that day and all night. The next morning, even though I was no longer sweating, I couldn't get up. I must have slept all day. I seem to remember Mary or one of the children checking on me from time to time. That evening, Mary brought me a bowl of matzo ball and chicken soup. It tasted wonderful. Suddenly, I looked up at her and said, "Where did you get the chicken?"

She said, "The Lord gave it to us." But as she said this, she glanced over at Jesus. I realized Jesus must have gone out and collected on some long overdue debts. It was wonderful soup!

I was in bed for several weeks and had my favorite soup with chicken every evening. One night when Simon brought it to me, I said, "Thank you, Simon. I believe I could eat chicken matzo ball soup forever and never get tired of it. Don't you just love it!"

"Yes, I do, but..." He turned his head away. Then it dawned on me that the family didn't have the chicken in their soup, only I did. So I whispered to him, "Hey, go get yourself a spoon and you can have some of mine." His eyes brightened and he rushed from the room and was back in the blink of an eye. We enjoyed the soup together.

The next morning I got up and helped a little in the shop. I couldn't do much, I just didn't have the strength. I watched Jesus working and helping James and little Joseph, who wasn't so little anymore. Simon came in and cleaned up some of the sawdust and shavings. Even tiny Judas was working. As I watched them all at work, my eyes began to blur. I had to leave. I stumbled back to bed and the tears came. I cried out to God, realizing I might not have many more days with my family.

Throughout the winter of my sickness, my friend James

came to visit regularly. He brought me news from the village and the countryside. He also brought me up to date on happenings at the synagogue, where he had recently become much more active. This was great news, and I listened attentively.

I hoped that when spring came I'd finally be my old self and be able to take up my work again. But with spring and the warmer weather, I only felt worse. James continued to visit me and try to cheer me up. Frankly, though, it only depressed me more as I compared his robustness with my growing frailty. I began to wonder if I would ever get well.

One day, James came carrying a large package. He often brought me little gifts, sometimes a chicken, since he knew I liked it so much—but he'd never brought anything this big. Jesus was with me when James arrived. He started to leave, thinking we would want to be left alone, but I spoke up and said, "Uh..., Jesus, you can stay if you like." He turned back.

Then James added, "Yes, please do."

After Jesus sat back down, James joined him. Still holding the package, he cleared his throat again and said, "Yes, well, uh, I have a confession to make." Jesus and I were puzzled, wondering what our best friend could possibly have to confess.

We said nothing, waiting for him to speak. This was a rarity in itself since he was never at a loss for words! Finally he seemed to collect his thoughts and said, "It's like this...many years ago I had a very good friend, actually more like a brother. He and I made a bargain." He looked down at the floor, frowning, "I traded him one cheap donkey for one of his most prized possessions. He was in need, but I really wanted the thing he had. I offered him two donkeys knowing he couldn't afford to keep two. I didn't offer him what he really needed and which I could afford...some gold in addition to the donkey." Pausing he looked over to Jesus, "The possession he was giving me was worth it, but I was too cheap in my heart to give it." Jesus looked back at James with compassion and sorrow.

I started to interrupt, but he raised his hand, looked up to the ceiling, then down to the floor and went on, "I even jokingly got him to promise to name his first son after me, which he gracefully agreed to do. And then he and his new wife left on a journey to Bethlehem."

He paused for a moment, then, "I've felt rotten about that ever since. I knew I hadn't done right by him and determined that as soon as he got back I'd make it right. But he didn't come back and that made me mad." Shaking his head, he added, "I thought he was just making me suffer for the way I treated him." He stood up, looking out the window, "Then I heard of the slaughter of all those babies in Bethlehem... I tried to locate my friend only to discover that he'd left town in the middle of the night. No one knew where he was or what condition he was in...I began to lose the hope of righting my wrong."

Sitting down with a sigh, he continued, "Next, my friend's wife's parents died of heartbreak because they, too, couldn't find their lost daughter, son-in-law, and grandson. How they were so certain there *was* a grandson, I don't know. Then we started hearing tales about my friend that I couldn't believe. But when put together with all the other strange happenings...well, they seemed possible." I looked away embarrassed as he stared directly at me. Getting my attentions again, he added, "So I hardened my heart toward my friend."

James paused, then continued, his voice thick. "Well, when he did show up, I was still mad. I only wanted to see if he had kept his part of the bargain." Softening his voice, "I had planned to forgive him of all his foolishness and apologize for not being a bigger help. But, when I found out he hadn't named his first son after me as he promised, I was furious."

He paused to catch his breath and I jumped in before he could stop me, "I remember that day!" I said. Jesus was nodding his head, like he was thinking, *I remember that, too.*

"Let me finish!" James said fiercely. "I knew in my heart I was wrong, but just couldn't bring myself to admit it." Clicking his tongue in frustration, "I let this go on for years. You went your way and I went mine. But that trip back from Jerusalem when you asked me to keep my namesake, I could hardly refuse. In those few days with little James I learned to love him like he was my own. By this time, I knew I was being downright silly and stupid, but my pride kept me from admitting my mistake, even when we renewed our friendship.

"Now, I want to return to you what is rightfully yours."

Of course, I had guessed what was in the package almost before he began his story. But before I could say anything, he continued, "I was completely wrong for taking advantage of you when you were in need. I'm sorry for listening to the tales that were told about you and especially for believing them. Will you forgive me for acting like a donkey and not a friend to the best friend I ever had?"

Tears were rolling down his face. I suppose his apology was the most difficult thing he had ever done.

With a full heart, I replied, "James, oh James, my

friend. My best friend. Brother! With rejoicing I forgive you for anything you might have meant for evil. I can assure you, though, that your giving me the one donkey was all the payment I expected."

"You always were bashful about asking a fair price for anything." he quipped.

"But I have a confession to make, as well." Now *he* was puzzled. I continued, "I did, honestly, name *my* first son after you."

"Then whose son is Jesus? Do you mean that Mary went..." He glanced at Jesus, closed his mouth, then looked at me, incredulously.

"That's a long story that you may have trouble believing. That's the reason I never told you before." And with that I told him a little of the story about Jesus and the trip to Bethlehem and the time in Egypt. I could not tell it all, but I tried to bring him up to our arrival back in Nazareth. From there, he pretty well knew the story.

When I finished, he said, "I don't know that I really understand it all, but...well, I determined, before God, that I would come over here, and I would trust you as my friend regardless of what happened. Whether you forgave me or not. Whew, but I never reckoned with a story like this!" He looked over at Jesus and mouthed the word, "Messiah?" Jesus just nodded his head, slightly.

I think James started to bow down, but I grabbed his hand and said, "James, Mary and I have kept this a secret, not because of the pain and difficulty it might cause us, but because God has shown us that it is His task to promote His own son. We don't want this to become known until God shows us His own plan. Okay?"

At that moment, Mary came walking into the room carrying two bowls of soup. "I suppose you men are hungry. You've been talking all day."

"Mary, look what James has brought us!" She, too, knew immediately what it was.

A big smile filled her face and she said, "James, you shouldn't have."

"Why doesn't someone open it? All of you have seen it, but I haven't." Jesus said.

I had forgotten—we had never told him about the cradle!

I motioned to him and said, "Why don't you open it, then?" He grabbed it and started ripping open the covering like he was a child instead of a young man.

When he got the wrapping off, he looked it over carefully, admiring the joints and the finish. There were a few scratches on it from the years of use in James's house, but it still looked wonderful. Jesus said, "Papa, this is the finest piece of workmanship I've ever seen. I can tell you made it, but I've never seen any of your other work look so exquisite."

"Son, I've never loved anyone so much as I loved your mother," I said, looking up at Mary, "and I still do. I made this as a special engagement gift and I can tell you, I spent many hours on it."

"Then you sacrificed it to make the trip to Bethlehem..." Jesus had tears in his eyes, too.

I just sighed, exhausted. "Jesus, you can take my soup, I'm too tired to eat it now." I heard them muttering something about tiring me out, but I just rolled over and went to sleep. As I did, I thought how very rich I was!

220

Explanations of Cultural and Extra-Biblical Ideas

1. Joseph is greater and more godly than usually thought.

I have a high opinion of Joseph due to his responses to God concerning the angel's messages.

Consider that Zachariah received a message from God about his son to be, John. Zachariah, in doubt, questioned the message and lost his voice for nine months. When an angel appeared to Mary, she too asked a question, but not in doubt. She then responded with the beautiful affirmation: "Behold, I am the servant of the Lord..."

Joseph received messages from God via an angel *four* times. Each time he did exactly what God wanted, without question or hesitation.

God called him "a righteous man" or "a just man."

2. What did Jesus know as a child?

When Jesus was a boy, was He omniscient? My idea is that he was not, and that, perhaps, omniscience was realized in him at His baptism. We do not know for sure, but if He did know everything as a child, it was somehow hidden. What we do know from scripture is,

> "Jesus grew in wisdom and in stature and in favor with God and all the people." (Luke 2:52)

And,

> "Even though Jesus was God's Son, he learned obedience from the things he suffered." (Hebrews 5:8)

It seems that if one knows everything, there is nothing to learn. Jesus, as a boy, was still God. However, we know from Philippians that Jesus lowered Himself to become a man. Philippians 2:7-8 says:

> "Instead, he gave up his divine privileges; he took the humble position of a slave and was born as a human being. When he appeared in human form, he humbled himself in obedience to God and died a criminal's death on a cross."

This could mean that Jesus was a normal boy, but without sin—which, of course, means he was abnormal.

3. Joseph's love for Mary.

Some doubt Joseph's deep love for Mary as it was not typical in that day.

During an interview with biblical scholar,

Dr. Alexandar Birviš[23] he said the following, "Joseph's unusual love for Mary is expressed in the scripture when he does not want to harm her. This was his thinking even when, for all he knew, she had had relations with another man."

Joseph's reaction would be amazing if it happened in our culture. In the days when marriage partners were chosen by the parents, it is even more unusual.

4. Was Mary a perpetual virgin?

Some church groups deny that Mary had other children. There are two repudiations to this, one cultural and one Biblical. The cultural one comes from Dr. Birvis˘ in Serbia. "According to Jewish thinking," he explained, "Joseph would have been an unblessed man if he had not had children of his own, especially a son. Joseph himself would have felt he was not blessed."

---

[23]Dr. Alexandar Birviš (1928-2015), professor emeritus, polyglot, Bible translator, pastor, and writer, the author of numerous books, articles and other publications, and translator of ten books of the Bible into Serbian from the original languages. Dr. Birvis was a Serbian Baptist preacher and a pastor of the First Baptist Church in Belgrade, Serbia for almost 50 years. He held (Hon.) DD (1991) from Gordon-Conwell Theological Seminary in the USA, and BA in Oriental studies (1961) and BTh (1953) from the University of Belgrade.

The more compelling reason is in Matthew 1:25. "But he did not have sexual relations with her until her son was born. And Joseph named him Jesus." I believe if God wanted us to know that Mary never had other children, He would have told us.

Though the scripture clearly refers to other children belonging to Joseph and Mary, some claim that these were nephews and nieces rather than their own children. To give a son or daughter to a relative or grandparent was not uncommon in that day, but one would think these would be given to family members who were better off financially than Joseph. Mark 6:3 also mentions the local people knowing Jesus' brothers and sisters.

Another mention occurs in Acts 1:14, "They all met together and were constantly united in prayer, along with Mary the mother of Jesus, several other women, and the brothers of Jesus." The word for brothers is adelphos, meaning 'from' and 'delphus,' the womb. (Strong's Concordance).

"'Brothers' and 'sisters' are the usual terms for siblings; a different term for more general 'kinfolk' (e.g., Romans 16:11) is not used with regard to Jesus' siblings." (Bible Background Commentary)

5. When did Joseph and Mary arrive in Bethlehem?

In the traditional Christmas story, Mary and Joseph arrive in Bethlehem just before Jesus was born. My break with that tradition comes primarily from Luke 2:6, *"While they were there,* the time came for the baby to be born." That indicates that they were in Bethlehem for some length of time before the birth. (See Mary's Time line below.)

6. Did anyone suspect that Mary was "with child" before marriage?

This is the issue regarding whether Joseph and Mary experienced any censure for the baby being conceived out of wedlock. I think that, though they expected it, it never happened. Here's the reason. When Jesus returned to Nazareth, early in His ministry years, as recorded in Luke 4:14-30, His message was rejected. Some of the people said, "Isn't this Joseph's son?" It seems to me that if there had been any inkling of Jesus' conception happening before the marriage of Joseph and Mary, it would have been said here to discredit Him. The census was, I believe, God's way of getting the couple out of Nazareth and into Bethlehem before any potential gossip could begin. Counting the time they spent in Bethlehem and in Egypt, it was possibly six years before the family returned to Nazareth.

7. Mary's time line.

Let's begin with the visit of the angel. Because of the mention of her relative, Elizabeth, Mary went to visit her, probably seeking some assurance and comfort about her situation. According to the angel Elizabeth was six months along. I believe that Mary left very soon, one or two days, after the angel's visit. At that time she could only stay with Elizabeth three months, as it would have been inappropriate in that culture for her to be in the house during the birth of John. Therefore, she was only three months along when she returned to Nazareth.

Luke 2:5 in the KJV text reads that she was "great with child." The NLT2 says, "obviously pregnant." Other translations have, "she was with child" or something similar. As I understand it, the Greek word used simply means *pregnant*, with no indication as to size.

Assuming this, then Joseph and Mary arrived in Bethlehem before Mary was "showing," as we would say.

8. How old was Joseph?

Several writers and artists picture Joseph as an old man when he and Mary became engaged. This was done to support the idea that Mary was a perpetual virgin. Thus, Joseph was pictured as too old to father children. There is nothing in the Scripture to substantiate an old or a young Joseph. It appears that since he is known as a carpenter, he was older than Mary. He also does not appear to be around at the time Jesus began His ministry. We do not know what happened to him, but it seems evident that Joseph died before Jesus began his ministry.

9. Then, how old was Mary?

Some want to picture her in her early teens, partly because some girls married that early, and most were "promised" even earlier. Evidently she had not been "promised," which was unusual. So I picture her as 17 to 19, more mature than most and protected by God. Regardless of her age, her maturity is shown first by her commitment to the angel's message, 'I am the Lord's servant...'

Other evidence of her maturity and older age, is her

trip to visit Elizabeth and the content of Mary's Song which contains several quotes from the Old Testament (Luke 1:46-55). Remember that at that time, girls were not given any formal education.

10. Did Joseph and Mary know who Jesus was?

Some question whether Joseph and Mary really knew who Jesus was. One comment on this was that they would not have been able to treat him normally if they had known.

But consider this fact: Mary, for herself, had physical proof since she knew she had not been with a man. Joseph accepted it on faith, just as we must.

End

To the Reader

May God bless your understanding,

May you, like Joseph, learn to trust Him,

Through the difficult times, may your faith grow

And may Jesus Christ rule your life.

GDC

Made in the USA
Middletown, DE
28 September 2022